"You're Willie... Why didn't I spot it sooner?"

The wonder in Con's tone confused Liz. "Willie Newman—Liz Newman! It's so obvious, now that I know."

"I was—"

"Why didn't you—"

They spoke together. "I was going to tell you tonight, Con."

"Do you know how often I've thought about you over the years? Why didn't you tell me who you were at the beginning?"

She trembled. "I was afraid. I thought you'd despise me."

"Why on earth would I do that?"

"I was so different from the others. You must have had a real laugh about me after—after we..."

"We made love on the beach one summer's night. What I don't understand is why I never saw you again, or why, when we met years later, you pretended we were strangers. Tell me, Liz. Why all the secrecy?"

CATHERINE SPENCER suggests she turned to romance-fiction writing to keep from meddling in the love lives of her five daughters and two sons. The idea was that she would keep herself busy manipulating the characters in her novels instead. This, she says, has made everyone happy. In addition to writing novels, Catherine Spencer used to teach English in British Columbia, Canada.

CATHERINE SPENCER

SPENCER

a lasting kind of love

Harlequin Books

TORONTO • NEW YORK • LONDON
AMSTERDAM • PARIS • SYDNEY • HAMBURG
STOCKHOLM • ATHENS • TOKYO • MILAN

Harlequin Presents first edition August 1986
ISBN 0-373-10910-5

Original hardcover edition published in 1986
by Mills & Boon Limited

CHAPTER ONE

LIZ Newman was outraged. Sexual harassment, especially that of the slap-and-tickle variety, was an insult no one should have to tolerate. Learning that two of her employees were suffering the indignity of it put the light of battle in her eye. She couldn't change the world, she couldn't even change the ape who was guilty in this particular instance, but she could and would see to it that none of her girls had to put up with his offensive behaviour again.

—Leaning forward, she buzzed her receptionist who did double duty as her personal secretary. 'Sheila, get me the president of Henderson Industries on the 'phone, will you?'

She sat back in the high executive chair and drew a deep breath. The president of Henderson Industries, as she very well knew, was Conroy Michael Henderson. Rich, beautiful Conroy whose father owned the pulpmill town where Liz had grown up; Conroy, boy wonder, who had so admirably filled the shoes of his older brother, killed in Vietnam; good old Con, legendary college basketball hero.

And the last time she'd spoken to him was twelve years ago, at night, on a beach in the Puget Sound, in high summer. The summer of her discontent; the summer of her greatest, most burning humiliation.

And now, thanks to Nadine Baxter, she was forced to let him back into her life, but only, thank God, through the safe anonymity of the telephone—that was, if Sheila ever managed to make the call.

Cradling the receiver on her shoulder, Liz swung around to face the view of harbour and mountains and went over the conversation she'd had with Nadine.

The girl was plump and cute and flushed with

indignation, and Liz had hurried to placate her. 'Tell me exactly what happened, Nadine, and I'll take care of it.'

'I was polishing the coffee table in the penthouse suite, Ms Newman—sort of bent *over* if you get my drift ...' The words were accompanied by a gesture which spoke volumes, pert breasts straining against the lilac-and-black striped smock, saucy little bottom waggling aloft. 'And he—the guy in the snazzy suit—he *pinched* me, on my ... well, you know! On my——'

'I can guess,' Liz had cut in drily. Sometimes it was hard, especially with someone of Nadine's temperament, to know how much she had provoked the incident. 'What happened next?'

'Well! I gave it to him but good. "Get lost," I told him. But he thought I was playing hard to get or something. Anyhow, the next thing I know, he sort of had me *pinned*—against the table. Man, my tights are shot! "Geez!" I told him. "I'm not one of your rich playboy types. Hands off!" You oughta make him pay for the L'eggs, they cost me a bundle, unless ... maybe the Agency, Ms Newman?'

'I'll take care of it.' They seemed to be the only words left in Liz's vocabulary. In truth, her mind was reeling with the realisation that it was one of Con's employees who was the perpetrator, though she was far from convinced the man was entirely to blame. Nadine was the sort of gregarious, *ripe* young woman who attracted such overtures. Maybe she had been unintentionally provocative, maybe not. 'And then?'

'Heck, I got my stuff together and left. Came straight over here to report him. Don't send me back there, Ms Newman, please. The guy's an octopus.'

She had to ask. 'Nadine ... is it possible that you encouraged this man—without meaning to, of course?'

Nadine had cocked her head to one side consideringly. 'I suppose it's possible,' she'd conceded, unconsciously imitating Liz's careful tone, then, in a swift reversal to her usual breezy style: 'But Wendy Parker didn't—she's not the type—and he came on to her as well.'

Liz had been thunderstruck. 'Wendy Parker? She was harassed, too?'

'You got it, Ms Newman.' Nadine's vigorous nod had almost disrupted the mechanized rhythm of her jaw as she molded bubble gum to the roof of her mouth before stretching it to a fine skin over her tongue. 'She doesn't go for making a fuss, so she didn't come to you, but she doesn't go to the penthouse suite any more, either. You don't believe me? Check with Mrs J.'

'Oh, I believe you, Nadine.'

The incident had raised Liz's ire. She felt as responsible for the women she employed as she did for the good name of her agency, and the knowledge that Henderson Industries was involved in this particular instance stiffened her resolve not to let the matter pass without comment.

Six months ago, she'd taken a perverse delight in snagging the Henderson contract. It represented a special milestone to her, an indication of how far she'd travelled along the competitive road to corporate success. Working *with* as opposed to working *for* the company that had once paid her a pittance was a private and very personal victory for her, even if the negotiations had been completed in an entirely impersonal manner, and even though there were no witnesses to her secret triumph.

But she was quite prepared to forfeit the arrangement. Liz Newman had needed Henderson Industries twelve years ago, poor benighted creature that she'd been back then; the WREN Agency suffered no such dependency. She and her company could cope with Henderson, or without them.

The intercom buzzed, penetrating the acrid fog of memory. 'Liz? Mr Conroy Henderson is on line two.'

Her voice was, as always, totally in control of the situation. 'Thanks, Sheila.'

She extended a perfectly manicured finger and

depressed the second button from the left. Settling the instrument more comfortably to her ear, she opened her mouth, afire with justified indignation, prepared to launch a blistering protest at the treatment meted out by one of his employees to one of hers.

Then panic descended out of nowhere, cementing her tongue to the roof of her mouth and paralysing her throat.

'Hello?' His voice, smooth and warm as melted chocolate, rolled across time like a caress. 'Hello WREN Agency?'

She clutched the receiver in both hands, one damp palm clamped protectively over the mouthpiece as though to prevent his watching her through the little holes perforated in its surface. Perspiration dewed her upper lip, her forehead, and sprang in a thousand tiny stings down her arms and behind her knees.

'He . . . llo?' Gently, encouragingly.

A tremor was starting, somewhere deep inside her, a place so secret and protected that not a soul knew of its existence. She'd almost fooled herself into believing that *she'd* forgotten about it. Until today. Until Nadine Baxter had burst into her office, puffed up with injured dignity, and given her cause to probe at old wounds that should have healed long ago.

It had taken years of careful layering—anger over the hurt, pride over the despair, indifference over the heartbreak—but in time, Liz had believed the composite result to be a true reflection of her emotional climate. It had taken less than a minute for Con Henderson to cut through the slick façade. The sound of his voice, deep and vibrant in her ear, exposed a single, unpalatable truth: of all the men in the world, only he could mount such a formidable assault on her atrophied sensuality and bring it flickering back to life. Underneath all her manufactured hatred, the knowledge of his power terrified her.

That the cool, poised, withdrawn Liz Newman, self-made business person extraordinary, could possibly be susceptible to the physical magnetism of any man, let alone Con Henderson, revealed a dismal lack of discipline. How dare that vapid other self emerge at such a time and crack her defences?

Quietly, defeat etched in tiny lines on her face, in the slump of her shoulders, she replaced the receiver. At least, she thought, he couldn't see me, though it's unlikely he'd recognise me after all this time.

The intercom sounded again. Collecting her briefcase and jacket, she crossed quickly to the door. Turning left, away from the reception area and the lifts, she skimmed down the hall to the heavy fire door and pushing it wide, took the flight of stairs to the floor below. There, safe from Sheila Johnson's curious eye, she punched the down button and, when it arrived, rode the lift to the ground floor of the building. Of course, she couldn't be sure, but she hadn't felt equal to taking the chance that the intercom message would inform her that her interrupted call had been reconnected. Not today. Not until she'd fortified herself for the attack, stoked up on bitter memories to arm herself against Con Henderson's intoxicating charm.

Wilhelmina Rowena Elizabeth Newman entered the panelled vestibule of the small, old-fashioned apartment building overlooking English Bay, and, shortly thereafter, into the restful elegance of her third floor apartment. Dropping the briefcase on a polished pedestal table of fine, inlaid rosewood, she passed through the entrance hall into the living room and went to stand directly at the window, where she leaned her forehead against the cold glass as though to revive herself from the numbing effects of admitting Con into her life again.

Behind her lay the tangible evidence of her success. British Indian rugs of palest ivory covered the expanse of soft-gleaming hardwood floors. Antiques, collected with love and care for almost a decade, graced the elegant proportions of the room in perfect harmony with the modern upholstered comfort of couches and chairs. Opposite the window, a white fireplace designed along classic Adam lines sported two Victorian daguerreotypes in plain oval mahogany frames over its mantel. Usually it all offered her unalloyed pleasure, but today, it had lost its power to charm ... to anaesthetise.

The October afternoon was sliding into evening, the sun hidden somewhere behind the low-lying clouds that draped the familiar outlook in gauzy grey, depriving the dcity of one of its more spectacular sunsets. She'd come to love Vancouver, the splendour that was British Columbia, though at first she'd hated them both. In the beginning, they'd represented an exile born of disgrace.

Impatient with her self-indulgent memories, Liz swung away from the window and marched purposefully into her bedroom. Flinging wide the closet doors, she systematically removed her outer clothing, consigning each item with neat precision to its appointed place: silk suit to padded hangers, blouse and tights to laundry hamper, shoes to cantilevered shelf.

Turning about, she faced herself in the full length cheval mirror and let the pale grey charmeuse teddy edged with fragile lace slither down around her ankles. The frown which had puckered her brow for the last hour gradually eased away as she surveyed the slender lines of her body. Raising one arm, she cleared the heavy, honey-coloured hair from her neck, noting with almost clinical interest how the gesture lifted her small, uptilted breasts and accentuated her narrow waist. Her gaze slipped lower, drawn to the scar on the left side of her abdomen, faded now to a thin, fine line. It was a significant reminder of the price she'd paid to know Con Henderson twelve years ago.

Such a tiny scar to conceal so much crushing hurt. And all because she'd let Con make love to her. First one doctor, hiding behind his official hospital greens, had told her kindly, clinically and quote firmly that the baby was gone; and then, weeks later, another had informed her she'd been left sterile. He'd explained it all with great patience and she had listened, her total incomprehension of such a vengeful fate cloaked behind a nodding acceptance of what was surely the ultimate cruelty.

But inside, something was screaming with pain. First, Con's defection, then the miscarriage, and now sterility. Was there no end to her punishment for having once transgressed? The accumulated anguish had torn at her self-worth. What was she, after all, but a useless, empty shell? Even rabbits could reproduce. But not Willie Newman.

Ironically, Liz had been conceived the very same day.

Raised by a mother whose expectations of decorum and conscience would have intimidated Emily Post herself, Willie had taken stock of her assets. Intelligent, law-abiding and normally tractable, she had, until her solitary and uncharacteristic impropriety with Con, been the sort who returned her library books before they fell due, who drove within the speed limit, who stopped to let little old ladies cross the road. She had been polite and respectful to her elders, even when they didn't deserve it, and she never put on underwear she'd have been ashamed to hang out on a laundry line.

And where had all these sterling qualities left her? Destitute, depressed, and barren, living proof that nice girls finish last. The fledgling Liz had learned her first lesson: the only person she could ever really count on was herself. It had spared her a lot of later grief; more to the point, it had helped her recognise her limitations and work around them. She had been, for a while, a very angry young woman, but no one would ever have guessed. However incomplete on the inside, to the world she presented a wholly secure and assured front. All the evidence of her pain, her scarring sense of utter worthlessness, were buried under the increasingly complex layers of her elegant disguises.

Everything had started to change—except for the scar. Nothing about that would ever alter.

Abruptly, Liz lowered her arm. Expertly cut, her hair fell in loose waves to her shoulders, gleaming like pale bronze against the fine, translucent skin. It was her thirtieth birthday, and she had a dinner date that evening with a charming and eligible bachelor. She was Liz Newman, secure and successful. People turned to look at her as they passed her in the street; men rushed to open doors for her, to pull out chairs. Slowly, painfully, and at great personal cost, she had acquired class, chic, pizzazz—call it what you will. She would not let Con Henderson alter that. Liz Newman was one of the beautiful people and Willie Newman was dead.

She'd hated the nickname, but it had clung relentlessly through high school, adopted by every last inhabitant of Cannon River, the small town on Washington's Puget Sound where she'd grown up. She'd despaired of ever shedding it, had entertained morose visions of herself at ninety, white-haired and incredibly wrinkled, known to a brood of irreverent descendants as Great Grandma Willie.

She'd pursued femininity, flaunting it, during her teens, shunning the tomboyish activities of her childhood. She had even sprouted the requisite number of rounded curves in all the right places, but the name had stuck, a plague to her vanity, an affront to her emerging sexuality. Con Henderson might, if he stretched his memory to extraordinary lengths, recall the name Willie and the colourless creature attached to it, through he'd never, in a million years, be able to associate a face, much less a body, with it.

Not that she'd been much to treasure in a young man's heart. It was a miracle, even to her, that the sleek lines she enjoyed today had evolved from the chubby adolescent with the braced teeth and the long hair ornamented with a thousand unsightly split ends. And the hands! As her mother had once pointed out with unusual acerbity, she could have shed five pounds if she'd only given up snacking on her nails!

No, Con would never associate the glossy Liz Newman with that other pathetic creature.

Con. Her heart turned over in splendid defiance at the memory of his voice earlier, spanning the years with such ease, opening old wounds, bathing her in futile longings. Con Henderson of the lazy cobalt gaze and thick black hair, of the long sensitive fingers, the warm persuasive mouth. Con Henderson, she reminded herself, shaken by her wayward emotions, of the casual 'love 'em and leave 'em' attitude. She recalled with painful intensity how ardently she had loved and how effortlessly he had left, and the memory served to ignite a flame of anger that burned cleanly, destroying the disturbing, dangerous thoughts of a man best forgotten.

When she opened the door to her escort, Jens Neilsen, an hour later, there was nothing about her to suggest that her cool poise had teetered on the brink of destruction. She was, as always, as expected, supremely elegant and just slightly withdrawn, alluring enough to tempt Jens to fantasise on the delights of her body, and reserved enough to render such yearnings unthinkable vulgarities.

It wasn't his fault. Blessed with intelligence, breeding and wit, six feet of pure Nordic charm, he was eminently suitable. His only deficiency was his inability to erase Con's indelible image from Liz's retentive mind.

Sheila was sorting mail with one hand and fielding incoming calls with the other when Liz gave her a wave of greeting as she passed through the reception area of the agency the next morning. Attempts by the receptionist to halt her employer's progress went ignored. Despite her determination to dismiss yesterday's abject cowardice, Liz felt unequal to explaining her sudden and furtive disappearance from the premises.

Secure in her office, she hung up the soft suede jacket that matched the tender green of her wool trousers and replaced it with a lilac striped smock, her customary uniform during office hours. The flashing red light of the intercom caught her eye a hair's breadth of a second before the buzzer heralded the end of the early morning calm. Wednesday always brought forth a flurry of social emergencies for the coming weekend and although Christmas was still twelve weeks distant, the agency's bookings were approaching the usual seasonal chaos.

'Yes, Sheila?'

'Mrs Franks is here for her interview, Liz. Would you like a few minutes longer before I send her in?'

'No need. I'll see her right away. Anything else?'

'Nothing pressing. Janice wants to see you later about some grand wedding reception at the University Women's Club, and Jim Lloyd from Midtown Toyota would like an appointment today if you have time.'

Liz ran her eye down her daily planner. 'Schedule him between two and three if you can.'

'Will do. That's it, then—unless there's anything else you need?'

Liz didn't know when she'd reached a decision and her reasons for it didn't bear close examination, but she had arrived at a solution for Nadine and her amorous pursuer. 'Just one thing more, Sheila. Draft a letter to Henderson Industries cancelling our contract with them.'

'Did you say *cancel?*'

'*That's what I said, Sheila.*'

'*Why . . . what reason shall I give?*'

Liz's sigh of exasperation gusted into the 'phone. 'I don't know. Think of something.'

'Okay.' Sheila's tone was cautious and Liz ran a distracted hand through her hair.

'Sorry, Sheila. It's shaping up to be one of those days, but I don't mean to take it out on you.'

'You're not. I'll get right on it and have a letter ready

for signature by the time you're finished with Mrs Franks.'

Sheila was her oldest employee; it was unforgivable to treat her so shabbily and not be able to offer any reasonable explanation for her behaviour. The trouble with hiding her lurid past from others, Liz decided, was the loneliness it occasionally incurred. Not very often, but sometimes, it would be a relief to confide in someone, and now was one of those times.

She couldn't approach her mother. Ellen seemed to have shut the door on anything but maternal love ever since she was widowed shortly after Liz's birth; shut it with such finality that it had always seemed a most indelicate intrusion for Liz to belabour her with her own problems.

Not that her mother would have been unsympathetic. She would simply have retreated into vague and gentle platitudes of comfort and unwittingly burdened Liz with guilt at having disrupted the serene flow of the older woman's life. To mention Con Henderson, even after this length of time, would fragment Ellen's calm brutally, forcing her to acknowledge that the heartache of loss and rejection could still taint her daughter's well-ordered fortress of success.

Liz found herself smiling at the prospect of confiding in her mother. Ellen, with her bridge club and her hospital volunteer work, insulated by the right friends and associates from anything that smacked of scandal. It would be heartless even to joke with her on the subject of Con.

There was a knock on the open door, and Liz glanced up to find a pale, exhausted-looking young woman hesitating on the threshold. Consigning Con to the past where he rightly belonged, she turned her attention to the more deserving case of Susan Franks, who, according to the file before her on the desk, was the single, near-destitute parent of two small sons. She was exactly the sort of case the WREN Agency liked to take on. Within six months, Susan Franks would be earning

enough money to afford a few frills, and would have
gained a measure of independence and confidence, too,
if Liz had anything to do with the matter.

Five days later, a benign sun chased away the remnants
of an early morning frost and coaxed the city into
revealing its natural beauty. Mountains dusted with
snow reared in proud magnificence to the north, while
the inlets and bays to the south and west threaded
ribbons of improbable blue between suburban shores
and busy harbour, swooping into sheltered yacht basins
and lapping city beaches.

It was enough, Liz thought, turning away from the
window and scanning the figures on the page before
her, to make a person dash out and do something
rash—like trade in the four decrepit Pintos that
provided the agency with transportation, for a fleet of
six sleek new Toyota station wagons. Jim Lloyd had
presented her with a tempting price package which,
weighed up beside the increasingly frequent and always
costly repair bills on the ancient Pintos, was not such a
wildly extravagant investment as she'd first supposed.

Grabbing up the sheet of information, she made her
way to the reception area, collecting Janice Raines on
the way. It was a good time for a joint conference;
Mondays were always slow, and Liz made a point of
including her two other office employees in as many
decisions as possible.

Settling themselves in the comfortable area around
Sheila's desk, coffee mugs at their elbows, the three
women pored over the figures quoted on the new cars.

'The price includes the logo as part of the custom
paint job?' Janice enquired.

'Everything—the name, the silhouette, even the
'phone number.'

'Great advertising. I say go for it, Liz, and I'm sure
the girls on the road would agree. God, I'm just waiting
for the day one of those jalopies empties its oily guts all
over some client's brick-paved courtyard. It's going to
cost us more in clean-up than the cars are worth.'

'And it's hardly the sort of service *we* can provide,' Sheila added. 'Parquet floors are one thing, but scrubbing interlocking paving stones ... that's heavy-duty commercial cleaning. What about trade-in value, Liz?'

'Forget it. Jim Lloyd can't offer us anything. He suggests we sell them for scrap and parts.'

She stood up to place her empty mug on the corner of Sheila's desk, and as she did so, the sheet of figures slid from her knee and fluttered erratically to the floor, finally coming to rest far under the two-seater couch on the opposite wall of the reception area. Dropping to her hands and knees, Liz bent down and reached out for the paper, unaware that, as she did so, the agency's outer door opened, giving the newcomer a delectable view of her neatly skirted bottom undulating gently in mid-air as she manoeuvred the paper free. 'Apparently, there's a fair demand for spare parts, ever since they were recalled to get their rear-ends fixed.'

She emerged victorious from her search and sat back on her heels to survey the other two whose faces were a study in confusion and suppressed mirth. Misreading their expressions, Liz continued, 'Remember about five years ago? Ford recalled the earlier models and fixed them so there weren't ... gas explosions ... in the event of——'

Janice erupted into a snort of merriment and Sheila made to rise from behind her desk, her bosom heaving in agitation.

'What ails you two?' Liz demanded.

'I think I do,' a voice replied, and at the sound of it, the blood seemed to drain out of Liz and seep into the carpet under her. A second stretched into painful infinity before she switched to automatic pilot and let her reflexes take over, but when a hand, warm and firm and masculine, reached from behind to grasp her elbow and assist her to her feet, reflexes fled and her knees threatened to sag.

Con Henderson was here, in her agency, inhaling the

same mass of purified, heated air as she. In fact, his breath was warm on the back of her neck.

Sheila, swift concern on her face, spoke first. 'Liz? Are you all right? You look . . . pale.'

'I'm fine.' Were those really her tones issuing forth with such calm assurance? Wrenching her mind under control, she turned slowly about, reaching one surreptitious hand behind her to lean for support on Sheila's desk.

Oh God! He was instantly recognisable, exactly as she remembered him. Long and lean, the wicked blue eyes fringed with outrageous lashes of such length they had clearly been intended to adorn female features, the thick hair black as coal, springing in lively defiance from his scalp with such energy that it seemed possessed of a life of its own.

For all his executive clout, he still retained the engaging approachability of his youth. Already, Sheila was bustling towards him, positively fluttering with motherly concern. 'Good morning, sir. May we help you?'

'I hope so. I'd like to see your boss, if he's around.'

'May I ask who——?'

'Forgive me.' He flashed a smile, loaded with such calculated charm that Liz was positive she could hear Janice salivating. 'I'm Con Henderson—and I wanted to discuss the letter I received last week.'

Sheila glanced hesitantly at Liz. 'Well . . .'

'I authorised the sending of that letter, Mr Henderson.' Scraping together the tattered remnants of her control, she willed her voice to convey cool neutrality. 'It was quite straightforward as I recall.'

'Painfully so——'

'If you've read your contract . . .'

'Ah yes, the contract. That's what I——'

'Then you'll be aware of the reciprocal clause whereby either party is free to cancel if the other is in violation of the terms of the agreement.'

'Exactly.' His tone was dry and—could it be?—

amused. 'Am I to infer from your well-rehearsed spiel that Henderson Industries is "in violation of the terms of the agreement"—whatever that means?'

'That's right, Mr Henderson. Good day.'

The air was being squeezed out of her lungs, all her insides aquiver, and she sensed Janice's and Sheila's open-mouthed astonishment at her high-handed treatment of such an important client. But she had to terminate the interview with Con before she collapsed.

Spine rigid, she swung away from him and marched down the hall and into her office. Painfully wheezing air into her constricted lungs, she leaned both palms flat on her desk and felt the leaden weight of asthmatic tension begin to ease, leaving her light-headed and exhausted.

But she'd done it. At last, after twelve years, she'd come face to face with him, dealt with him, and dismissed him. He hadn't recognised her and that, too, was a victory of sorts. If Willie had been too bland to bear remembering, Liz had left a lasting, albeit unfavourable impression. He surely wasn't used to having his authority flouted, even less accustomed to a woman's indifference to his practised charm.

And that reminded her: Sheila and Janice hadn't helped much, drooling on the sidelines like a pair of witless teenagers. She'd have a few choice words for them later.

And then, just when her breathing was approaching normality: 'If you're so certain you have a case, you'll surely take a few minutes to explain it to me?'

Her heart leaped into her throat, thudding violently and choking off her newly established source of air. Casting wildly about for an avenue of escape and finding none, she turned like an animal at bay. He lounged in the doorway, flat leather briefcase tucked under one arm, the jacket of his charcoal grey business suit unbuttoned to reveal the sober waistcoat beneath. No doubt about it, he was the very essence of corporate success, from the tips of his hand-made Italian leather shoes to the gold Rolex on his wrist.

'I find the subject distasteful.'

'Then perhaps someone else, Miss . . .'

'Newman, Liz Newman.' She watched carefully, but the name registered nothing on his face.

'I believe I'm entitled to an explanation, Ms Newman.'

Had he heard 'Liz' as 'Ms'? she wondered distractedly, then forced her mind back to the real issue confronting them.

She shook her head in a gesture of defeat. 'Very well, I'll spell it out for you. This agency does not tolerate sexual harassment towards its employees under any circumstances, and that is why our contract with your company has been terminated.'

It sounded melodramatic, even to her ears, but with what she hoped was an air of unmistakable finality to the discussion, she turned from him, seated herself behind the desk, drew forward a letter awaiting her attention and immersed herself in the absorbing news that the latest steam-cleaners for carpets ejected a lethal shot of flea killer into home furnishings, thereby keeping pets and their owners parasite free.

The briefcase, which only moments earlier had lodged so comfortably under his arm, suddenly flopped with considerable force on to the desk. Only by dint of extraordinary self-control did she refrain from flinching at the impact.

'Sexual harassment, how?' He sounded more astonished than disbelieving, but there was a steely bite to his voice that had not been there before.

'I'd prefer to avoid the specifics.'

'Well, I wouldn't, because whether or not you accept this, Ms Newman, my company isn't too all-fired in favour of it either, and if someone working for me is dishing out that sort of crap, I want to know about it. So, let's hear the rest.'

He had drawn up a chair close to the desk and was seated now with his forearms only inches away from where her nerveless fingers were splayed across the letter.

Keeping her eyes firmly on the alien briefcase, she began to speak. 'Two of my girls have been subjected to the ... er ... unwelcome overtures of a young man who seems to have some sort of connection with your entertainment suites in Harbour House. I can't give you his name because I don't know it and I won't reveal the identities of my employees who have suffered enough embarrassment already.'

'No need.' He was plainly disturbed at her disclosure. 'And I'll find out who the culprit is *today*. Why in the world didn't you just call up and make a direct complaint? Did you think it would be ignored or disbelieved?'

The ensuing pause made it clear he expected a reply and with reluctance, she raised her eyes from their safe contemplation of the unremarkable briefcase, and steeled herself to meet his curious gaze. 'Well?'

'I—er ... it didn't seem ... it's not the sort ...' Her pitiful attempt to explain her utterly illogical manner of dealing with the situation trickled into embarrassed silence.

'Ms Newman?' The straight black brows were raised in amused disbelief. 'Surely I'm not to understand that a woman of your obvious capabilities found such a task beyond her?'

A flush of annoyance stained her cheeks. She hadn't come this far as an independent businesswoman by cowering in a corner every time something unpleasant cropped up. Normally, she would have reacted as forthrightly as he'd suggested, suffering no qualms about how her complaint would have been received. Normally, her heart didn't race at the sound of a client's voice; normally, she didn't find herself remembering the texture of a client's skin, or the spiralling response of her own body to his touch.

But how to convey this without sounding slightly deranged? The truth was out of the question. Not for the world would she reveal to him that she had started to 'phone him, that his simple 'Hello?' had flung her

back to the summer she was eighteen and left her
suspended somewhere between the aching memory of
cool moonlight on naked limbs, warm lips and gentle
hands seducing her into regrettable surrender, and the
fear that, given the opportunity, she might repeat the
same mistake over again. How did the old saying go?
Fool me once, shame on you; fool me twice, shame on
me!

Marshalling every ounce of self-discipline, she met his
gaze with a commendable show of composure. 'Forgive
me, Mr Henderson. I obviously underestimated your
company's code of ethics. Unhappily, not everyone
shares your enlightened view of the problem. I'm
impressed that you took time from your busy schedule
to take care of the matter personally.'

He grinned suddenly, his teeth white and even, and
admitted with engaging frankness: 'Well, I didn't
exactly do that. I'm on my way to a meeting on the
fourteenth floor and just happened to notice your
agency's name on the directory downstairs. I recognised
it because my business manager had brought your letter
to my attention just this morning. She's in quite a
state—apparently you offer great service. I hope I can
tell her the problem's been straightened out and that
we're back in business as usual?' At her doubtful
expression, he hurried to reassure her: 'I've a pretty
good idea who's at the bottom of this and you have my
word there'll be no further incidents.'

'As you wish, Mr Henderson. We'll pick up where we
left off.' It was a grossly inaccurate response, all things
considered, but anything to get him out of her office.
Every time she made contact with the blue intensity of
his glance, her heart lurched and it was all she could do
to keep from letting her eyes roam the well-remembered
contours of his face, a physical effort to keep her hands
primly folded on the desk in front of her and not let
them follow on a tactile tour of their own.

Mercifully, he rose to his feet, gathering up the
briefcase and shooting a quick glance at his watch.

'Then I'm glad I stopped in. It's been a real pleasure, Ms Newman. I wish I had more time, but I'm already late for my next appointment.'

Her relief froze into shock, however, as he extended his well-shaped hand across the desk. The contact was brief but charged with such electricity that she was amazed not to find on her skin a permanent imprint of his clasp.

He made as if to leave then changed his mind and swung back to face her. 'What time do you usually eat lunch?'

His question, fired out of nowhere, halted her plummeting spirits and caused them to soar like a demented yo-yo. 'Lunch?'

He imprisoned her in that careless, utterly charming grin, depleting her reserve of caution. 'Lunch,' he affirmed, 'in, say, an hour? Let's make it twelve-thirty. I'll stop in on my way down from my meeting.'

'Oh no! Really, you don't have to——'

'I'd like to. Anyway, it strikes me we should discuss our problem further, make sure circumstances don't permit a repeat. We have a responsibility, wouldn't you say, to our employees? Do us both a favour and let me make amends for the problems we've caused you.'

'Well, all right.' Crazy, crazy lady, to be made so foolishly happy by a man so patently hard to resist, so impossible to forget. 'But I'll meet you downstairs in the foyer.' If she was going to make a fool of herself, she'd prefer not to have witnesses.

'In the foyer then, at half-past twelve.'

CHAPTER TWO

AFTER the door had closed behind Con, she had slumped at her desk, nostalgic regret for what might have been flooding her senses. Twelve years was a long time in anyone's life and for her, they'd been the years when her friends and peers had formed serious relationships, made lasting commitments, married, had babies, while she had pursued success, believing that for her, the other dreams were over.

She was, if nothing else, pragmatic. Some day, she hoped to marry; some day when the challenge of business began to pall, when the loneliness of old age loomed with more immediate threat. Some nice man would come along who would need her for the things she *could* give: a widower, perhaps, or a divorcé, with a brace of handsome sons starved for the gentling influence of a mother-figure; or a pretty, vivacious daughter who'd provide Liz with all the vicarious thrills of motherhood.

Now, she realised how foolish she'd been. Con was impossible to forget, to replace. Love, emotional commitment, weren't like a business. They had direction and desire beyond the control of an alert and organised mind.

Why couldn't things have turned out differently? Was it really too fantastic that Con should have returned her love, despite the disparity in their upbringing? Had she really been such a colourless nobody that she'd passed through his life and left not one single lasting impression? And if the answers to both questions were yes, then why couldn't she have been the sort of girl who went on to find newer and greater love, instead of being the once-in-a-lifetime type? For if he'd accomplished nothing else by bursting back into her life, Con had proved inexorably that her passion for him was as sure and strong and permanent as the tides sweeping up the Gulf of Georgia or the mountains standing sentinel over the city.

And yet, what good were all these yearnings? That the rest of the world saw only the capable, glamorous Liz Newman whose life was as orderly and successful as her business didn't alter her knowledge of herself. Outward appearances to the contrary, underneath all the gloss, she was empty: emotionally arid; physically barren; sexually irrelevant.

She was, she'd decided at one point in her mid-twenties, probably frigid. That was undoubtedly why she found the hungry fumblings of her incipient suitors so repellent. When they, the men of medicine, had taken away her ability to reproduce, they'd severed some vital emotional connection to passion, too. Having, therefore, accepted herself as an incomplete woman, she was thoroughly confused—disgruntled even—to discover that Con, by the merest whisper of an impersonal finger on her skin, could revive the painful longings of her youth; could resurrect anew her grief at being unable to tap that vast reservoir of blighted maternal instinct she'd smothered for so many years.

Enough! she decided. Quite simply, she could not be like other women. She was only half complete, a fruit fallen from the tree too soon. And no amount of wishing or whining could change that.

Her impatience with herself showed in the vigour with which her chair careered away from her desk as she rose. The past was interfering altogether too much with the present. Clamped once again in the iron jaws of efficiency, she strode down the hall to the reception area. It had taken an hour but she'd recovered enough to face her staff again.

'The contract still stands, Sheila, so make sure we have someone over at the Henderson penthouse on Friday. It might be a good idea to send two people instead of one.'

'I'm glad you got it all sorted out,' Sheila replied, satisfaction evident in her comfortable smile. 'It would have been a pity to lose the contract and he's such a *personable* fellow. You know, I'd somehow expected him to be a lot older. He can't be more than about thirty-two or three.'

'Thirty-five actually,' Liz responded, and could promptly have cut out her tongue at her indiscretion.

'Really? How do you know?'

'I read it some place—can't remember where.'

'Imagine that. Is he married?'

'That I don't know.' She forced herself to adopt a vague, distracted tone and pretended to scrutinise the appointment book on Sheila's desk. But a cold fist of apprehension slammed into her solar plexus. *Was* he married? She'd memorised every word the media had ever issued, but there was always a conspicuous absence of personal detail in any references to Con. Like the rest of the Henderson clan, he was a very private person outside the area of his professional concerns.

She had always assumed that, if there had been a wife, her name or face would have appeared before now. It was not only logical but more comforting to cling to such an assumption. Yet, with the recent memory of him washing over her, how, she wondered, could he have escaped being snagged in matrimony? Vancouver was full of attractive, eligible women and surely one of them must have succeeded where doubtless thousands of others had failed.

The realisation caused such dull agony within that Agency concerns soured like old milk on her tongue. 'I think I'll take an early lunch, Sheila. My next appointment isn't until three and I need a change of scene. Don't expect me back too soon.'

Ignoring the surprised lift to her secretary's brow, she returned to her office to shed the smock in favour of the soft suede jacket, scooped up her purse and arrived at the lift just as one stopped at her floor on its downward journey.

It was twenty minutes to one when she stepped into the lobby. She was instantly conscious of Con's electric blue gaze sweeping over her from his position near the directory. It wasn't just his height that made him stand out; there seemed to be a sort of magnetic spark that leapt from him to her, bringing all her nerve endings raw and tingling to the very surface of her skin. A flood of warmth swept over her, leaving a chill of heightened awareness in its wake.

She'd half considered breaking her date with him, decided that to do so would be immature and inordinately rude, and was nevertheless plagued with doubt at the wisdom of her decision as she crossed the floor towards him. The cursory glance of recognition she had flung his way as she left the lift had made serious inroads into her hard-won equilibrium and she wan't sure she could endure any more of his company today. Having starved for so long, she feared now that too rich a diet of Con after years of deprivation was considerably more than she could handle.

Panic lent hesitation to her step, yet when his voice at her shoulder united with his hand at her elbow, her blood sang.

'Hey, we're going to lunch, not an execution,' he teased. 'I promise it won't be too unbearable.'

She turned to face him, a bloom of pure joy illuminating her features, dispelling uncertainty. 'Mr Henderson?'

'I thought,' he smiled down at her, the ridiculous lashes shading his eyes from the bright October sunshine bouncing off the glass towers of the downtown core as they emerged into the street, 'that we'd go some place special. I'd really like to polish my company's rather tarnished image.'

'That's not necessary.'

'I know.' He ogled at her charmingly. 'But accept anyway.'

It was insanity even to consider complying. It was

emotional suicide. 'Put like that, how can I refuse you?'
She positively sparkled at him.

'Wonderful! I knew you were a woman of good sense
the moment I laid eyes on you.' Magically, he had
commandeered a passing taxi and, a hand at her back,
swept her down to the curb and into the confining
intimacy of its back seat. 'Verezanno's, Granville
Island,' he directed the driver, then leaned back in his
corner once again to survey her with his lazy blue
regard.

A flush began at her toes and swept up the length of
her body at the unabashed admiration of his scrutiny,
halting at last in rosy confusion in the hollows of her
cheekbones.

Good God, he realised, she's actually blushing. I
thought that was a lost art. Aloud, he asked, 'You do
like seafood?'

'Love it,' she assured him and crossed her long and
rather lovely legs, determined to savour every last
minute of this unexpected and forbidden treat.

Shifting slightly, she turned to face him and the silken
rustle of hidden lingerie drew his gaze back to the
elegant display of limb from which he had, in the
interests of good manners, withdrawn his reluctant and
admiring observation. He was acting like a damn fool,
he decided, as hot and bothered at the prospect of
sneaking a look at a little lace as a schoolboy. But she
was an arresting sight, a symphony of spring greens and
delicate bronze, the stockings clinging to her legs
echoing the subdued fire of her hair drawn back to
reveal the perfect oval of her face. He was shockingly
tempted to reach out and run a hand over the silken
curve of her calf, but the patina of cautious reserve that
encompassed her was deterrent enough to stifle such
action. He knew instinctively that here was no brash
female executive; under the cool competent exterior
lurked a shy, tentative creature who would take flight at
the slightest hint of aggression from him. Easy,
Henderson, he cautioned himself, this one's different.

At his age, with his assets, he was fully cognizant of and not a little bored with the acquisitive gleam so often perceptible in the female eye as it examined him. Yet, Liz seemed impervious to his supreme eligibility. Was it possible she didn't care? Or was she already spoken for, promised to some other equally high-powered tycoon? Slyly, he stole a glance at her hands and noted with a discerning eye for detail not only that she did not sport a ring, but that her hands were as soft and white as petals, the nails shimmering pink, perfect ovals. What on earth was she doing running a cleaning service when, clearly, the closest she came to soap and water was relaxing in a scented bathtub?

'Tell me about yourself,' he invited, as the taxi pulled on to the Burrard Street Bridge and left the congestion of downtown behind. 'What got you started in your particular line of business?'

She could almost feel the shutters rolling down her face, closing him out as effectively as a wall. Carefully, she erased the panic from her eyes, denying the urge to turn away from his curious gaze and forcing herself to regard him with a façade of composure.

Careful, she warned herself, this is a loaded question, but he doesn't know it. 'Let's say I'm interested in working with underprivileged women,' she replied lightly.

'By employing them to clean up the mess left by other people? Isn't that treason in the eyes of Women's Lib?'

'Not at all. It's turning well-learned skills into lucrative art. My employees do a lot more than scrub floors and empty ashtrays.'

'I'm fascinated,' he told her, his eyes brilliant in the reflected waters of False Creek as the taxi slid to a halt on the dock outside Verezanno's. 'I want to hear more.'

Not if I can help it, she was tempted to retort. From here on, I'll ask the questions.

He was not, however, that easily deterred. No sooner were they seated upstairs at a window table—he was greeted with deferential cordiality by everyone from the

hostess to the waiter, she noticed; he was obviously well
known here—than he raised the subject again.

'So,' he continued, barely glancing at the menu
before laying it aside, 'you elevate ordinary housewives
to state-of-the-art domestics.'

He was joking, she knew, but she bristled anyway,
longing to sting him with a reminder of how
comfortable his life had been made by the luxury of
servants. 'I consider housewives to be "state-of-
the-art" period, Mr Henderson. They're a vastly
underrated part of our society,' she replied stiffly.
'What I *do* try to accomplish is to give them the
dignity of independence.'

'Aha! A Women's Libber after all.'

'Not,' she insisted, 'in the sense you mean. I don't
encourage my girls to march around Stanley Park
bearing placards proclaiming their unhappy lot in life.'

He chortled appreciatively at her succinct rebuttal.
'Then what's all this about "independence"? Isn't that
encouraging rebellion against us poor unsuspecting
men?'

'*Poor? Unsuspecting?*' she scoffed. 'It may interest
you to know, Mr Henderson——'

'Con,' he interjected.

'What?'

'Con—as in Conroy. I think we can safely progress to
a first name basis now that we've known each other
almost three hours.'

'Yes . . . well, as I was saying . . .'

'Con.'

For the life of her, she couldn't say it. Its familiarity
evoked such potent memories of half-hearted, whispered
protests on that long-ago, deserted beach. *Con, please
. . . please.* Protests? Who was she fooling?

'Try it, *Ms Newman.*' The lashes dropped low over
the vibrant blue of his eyes as he tilted his head
quizzically, a humorous lilt in his voice.

'Liz,' she conceded, a hint of laughter rising in
answer, and managed to overcome the ridiculous

hurdle. 'And as I was saying, I deal mainly with women who, for one reason or another, have been abandoned or mistreated by the very men who once vowed to cherish and protect them; women who have neither the money nor the time to invest in pursuing a new career.'

'But isn't it a rather demeaning way of earning a living?'

'It all depends on your point of view. If you see women as mindless drudges, then yes, I suppose it is. If being dependent on welfare or court-imposed support from a reluctant spouse is preferable, then again, the answer is yes. On the other hand, if you take the skills these women have often spent years acquiring, and show them how to perfect and enlarge on them, then you're giving them the tools to be useful, contributing members of the work force—no small feat in this age of mass unemployment.'

Con raised a finger in the direction of their waiter who promptly materialised at his elbow. 'Bring a bottle of the Chardonnay Reserve, '79,' he requested, then turned his attention back to her. 'Yes,' he said seriously. 'I see what you mean. Rather than see their years of home-making as wasted, you're elevating them into a source of income and pride—and doing it rather well, by all accounts.'

'Thank you. I'm amazed at the demand for our services, considering the general economic picture.'

'It's always the same: people will hang on to their luxuries at any price. I guess they're what help us all get through the rough times.'

Their wine arrived and for a moment he was occupied with examining the label and tasting the contents of the bottle. Satisfied, he leaned across the table. 'Will you let me order for both of us?' he asked. 'There are a couple of specialities not on the menu that I think you'd enjoy—that is, if you were being honest about liking seafood.'

'Go ahead. I like to be surprised occasionally.'

Following a brief discussion with their waiter, Con

raised his glass to her. 'Here's to the WREN Agency and its formidable founder.'

'Oh dear!' she gasped, almost inhaling the wine she was about to sip. 'Is that really how I come across? As for*mida*ble? Heaven forbid I should be so daunting!'

'You're anything but that, but I'd guess from what we've just been discussing and from our earlier exchange that you're rather protective of your employees.'

'Well, most of them have been through a lot and a couple have come perilously close to despair over their situations.'

'Tell me, did you start out as a social worker or are you carrying on a family concern, like me?'

There it was again, that deceptively innocuous curiosity that, honestly satisfied, would open a Pandora's Box of troubled secrets.

'Neither,' she answered briefly and, with relief, observed their waiter bearing down on them with their lunch. Pointedly changing the subject, she took advantage of the occasion to comment, 'I gather you're a regular here, what with the window table at a moment's notice and access to special items on the menu.'

A platter of Japanese delicacies arranged with austere intent to please both eye and palate was placed before them, the convoluted whorls of sculpted carrots and radishes a splash of colour against the black and white *sushi*. Side bowls of chilled *sunomono* completed the first course, wooden chopsticks angled precisely over the rim of each dish.

'Fairly regularly,' he agreed non-committally and she wondered again if there was a wife in the background, or some other special woman.

Worry about it later, she decided. For now, enjoy the moment. 'It looks wonderful.'

'Taste it first,' he advised, dazzling her anew with his smile. Twirling noodles expertly around his chopsticks, he glanced about the room, crowded now with a noisy lunch hour clientele. 'You can see I'm not the only one who likes the food, but I have to admit to a fondness for the competition down the road. Some time we'll go there and you can give me your unbiased verdict as to the better choice.'

A rush of joy raced through her blood, heady as wine. *This* time, there was going to be a *next* time.

The meal progressed at an easy, leisurely pace, the Japanese course being followed by scallops marinated in lime juice and, last, a sinful French pastry artfully concocted of airy layers of chocolate, cream, Cointreau, and candied violets.

It was over coffee that her poise almost forsook her. Mellowed by the ambience of the elegant mirrored restaurant, the unusual sequence of events that had brought Con back into her life assumed the warmth of a benison and she forgot to be careful.

He regarded her over the rim of his cup, the laughing blue eyes squinting in mild puzzlement. 'At the risk of sounding trite,' he remarked, lowering his cup to its saucer, 'haven't we met somewhere before today?'

She blanched, her aplomb evaporating. 'Positively not!' Oh dear, that was far too swift and emphatic. But how could she possibly skewer him with a coolly amused glance and suggest by a gently reproving laugh, chin propped on delicately extended forefinger, that his question was too gauche to merit further response, when she had to clench her hands and bite severely on her lower lip to curb their respective trembling?

He shrugged. 'Some social event, perhaps? The Symphony Ball? The opening of the new art gallery?'

'I think not, though your name is, of course, familiar. Perhaps our business connection is what *you* have in mind, too.' She forced herself to relax, uncurling her tight fists to her instant regret, for the slight movement captured his attention.

'You have the most extraordinarily beautiful hands,' he exclaimed, taking one of hers in both of his, and, turning it back and forth, examined the soft skin, the smooth and slender fingers, the impeccable nails, 'which brings me back to my earlier question: how does a woman like you learn about operating a maid service?'

'Bitter experience,' she replied, mesmerised by the dry warmth of his touch, his gentle fingertip exploration of the lines criss-crossing her palm.

'You a maid? With hands like these?' The sensory delight stopped suddenly. 'I don't believe you!'

Aware of her near blunder, she attempted to pull her hand free only to find it more securely imprisoned. 'I— no, not now, that is . . .'

Desperately, she gathered her scattered wits and tried again. 'The idea just came to me one day, and at first I went out on assignment because I had only a very small staff.'

He gave her hand a final squeeze then relinquished it. 'I like everything I've heard,' he remarked, the gleam in his eyes suggesting he was far from displeased with what he saw, either.

'What do you do when you're not rushing to the defence of hapless ladies?'

She should have reprimanded him for treating her staff so lightly, but the teasing smile, the gentle laughter in his eyes made it impossible for her to take offence. 'Nothing very interesting, so let's talk about you for a change,' she countered, hoping to divert his attention. 'When does the busy chief executive of a company like Henderson's find time for relaxation?'

'Not often enough,' he admitted. 'I seem to spend an inordinate amount of time on planes. It's a great way to wade through the paperwork, but it makes for a rather fractured social life.'

'You must have a very understanding wife,' she offered with what she prayed was a convincingly off-hand air. Under cover of the table, her hands knotted together and she braced herself for his answer.

'I don't,' he replied cryptically, and signalled for the bill. Reaching into an inside breast pocket, he withdrew a credit card and tossed it on the table, then raised his eyes to meet her uncertain gaze. 'I'm not married.' His voice was curiously flat and lacking in emotion, but elation filled her fearful heart.

Stepping on to the dock outside the restaurant, they paused for a minute to savour the beauty of the day.

'It's some sight,' he commented, gesturing to the backdrop of mountains and water. 'Watch your step,' he cautioned her, as they negotiated the planked boards and turned to the taxi stand, but her consciousness was filled with his touch, her senses joining forces and abandoning the far reaches of her body to congregate in quivering awareness at the angle of her elbow where his fingers took a firm hold to steady her. 'There's a free cab just drawn up.'

He was sublimely indifferent to the tempest his touch was creating, quite unaware that it left her weak with private ecstasy.

Twenty minutes later, he was gone and she was flung back into the unenchanted routine of the agency, striving with the utmost difficulty to drag her mind earthward, to concentrate on the business at hand. Was the purchase of the new Toyotas justified? Could the Pintos possibly last another six months? How could the simple touch of Con's hand be such a shattering experience when she'd know the far greater arousal of his most intimate caresses, surrendered to him as she had to no other man—been briefly pregnant with his child?

CHAPTER THREE

CON did not call during the days that followed. There were no more meetings, no more impromptu invitations. Liz, ignoring the hollow ache of wanting, refused to acknowledge how deeply affected she was by this second rejection; denied absolutely the tiny hope that had flickered briefly as a result of their lunch together. What was the point of hoping for a relationship based on a deliberate deception?

She was not, after all, prepared to regale him with an account of their first meeting, boosting his already considerable ego with the details of how she had offered herself to him, the proverbial virgin sacrificing her all for love. The mere idea of such a confession stoked the embers of her anger—anger which, considering how *justified* it was, seemed altogether too inclined to retreat in favour of tentative, pulsing hunger whenever Con entered her thoughts.

She reinforced her flagging spirits with frequent reminders that she was still in possession of those things that mattered: the success, the independence, the glamour. She reminded herself even more often of what she'd learned so long ago: how treacherous Con was, how uncaring.

A week passed, then two, and miraculously his image began, if not to fade, then at least to recede during working hours. If his azure eyes disturbed her dreams, she refused to admit it, denied the memory of his touch left her sleepless and desolate. The cool, passionless Liz was uncomfortable with such happenings.

On the Friday of the second week, sudden pandemonium descended on the Agency at a time when the hectic pace normally slowed into a pre-weekend lull.

Susan Franks was shaping up nicely. She was hard-working, pleasant and reliable and Liz felt she'd made a good choice in hiring her. She knew how desperate Susan was for the work, how far her salary had to stretch to feed her two small sons and pay rent on her basement apartment.

So, when Mrs Alicia Porter 'phoned in to report that Susan had suffered an accident while working in the Porter household, Liz was more than slightly concerned.

'What sort of accident?' she enquired anxiously, envisioning all manner of horrifying possibilities. The house was a Victorian mausoleum of a place, high-ceilinged and cursed with unexpected stairs in odd places.

'Oh my dear, I'm afraid it's my fault, or at least, Mr Chieng's.' Mrs Porter, Liz seemed to recall, was a gentle creature probably in her mid-fifties, a little overweight and, if her breathless agitation was any indication, probably suffering from asthma or high blood pressure. 'I really think she needs hospital care, but she won't listen to me. She insists on trying to continue with her work.'

Liz experienced a lightening of the dread that had settled on her at first hearing the news. Presumably, Susan was conscious and able to speak. If anyone was going to require hospitalisation, it would be Mrs Porter who was building up a dangerous head of steam and rapidly losing the power of rational thought.

'I'll come right over,' she promised, 'and we'll take care of Susan. Meanwhile, try not to worry.' Futile words, but the only comfort she could offer at the moment. Susan was undoubtedly pitting her injury against the cost of time off from work, and deciding she could ill afford the latter. A familiar anger at the vulnerability of single parents gnawed at Liz.

'Oh, thank you, dear. I'm here alone just now, you see. Both my husband and my housekeeper are out.'

'Fifteen minutes, Mrs Porter, that's all it'll take.

You'll manage 'till I get there. Just stay by Susan and try to get her to sit down.'

Hurriedly giving Sheila a run-down on the situation, she collected the Agency's first aid kit and made her way by taxi to the Porter mansion, located in the oldest residential suburb in the city. It was an area of tree-lined 'Crescents' and 'Drives', the imposing homes inhabited by 'old' money, revered city fathers. No brash numbering of anything so common as streets here.

Liz's memory had not played her false. Alicia Porter was short and dumpy, endowed with several chins that quivered with concern as she led Liz to the big, old-fashioned kitchen. Susan, a towel wrapped around one hand, and nursing a swollen ankle, sat at a table in the middle of the room.

'What happened?' Liz forced herself to stay calm, though when she removed the cloth covering the gaping wound to the palm of Susan's hand, a tremor of alarm shot through her. Mrs Porter was right: the young woman did need treatment and Liz only hoped the damage was superficial, and hadn't affected tendons or nerves.

'I've always been a klutz,' Susan offered shakily. Her skin felt clammy and chilled. Shock, Liz decided, remembering the first aid course she'd taken a few years earlier.

'Oh child, I hold myself entirely to blame.' Mrs Porter hovered anxiously at Liz's shoulder, regarding the injury fearfully. 'I should have kept Mr Chieng locked up, or at least warned you about him.'

'Mr Chieng?' Fatigue and concern, combined with the decidedly Gothic architecture of the house, played tricks with Liz's imagination. Shades of Jane Eyre, she thought a trifle giddily; the lunatic escaped from the attic and attacked poor Susan!

'My Pekinese. He has a habbit of getting underfoot, you see, and Mrs Franks tripped and hurt her ankle—and cut herself on the decanter.'

'I broke it,' Susan explained apologetically. 'I'm sorry, Ms Newman, but I'll pay for the damage.'

'I won't hear of it.' Mrs Porter was adamant. 'You weren't at fault.'

'Never mind, we'll sort it out later.' Liz could see that if she didn't put an end to the self-recriminations, the injuries would never receive the treatment they clearly needed. 'Where's your coat, Susan? We need to get you down to the General Hospital to get your hand seen to.'

It was seven-thirty when Liz finally let herself into her apartment, having shipped a sutured, injected Susan home by taxi. Lord, but she was tired. The day seemed to have lasted twenty-four hours already, but at least Susan's injuries hadn't been too serious.

Entering the living room, she lifted the 'phone off the hook and thankfully eased off the shoes she'd worn since morning, relishing the feel of the cool, smooth wood under her feet. Tonight, dinner would be a tin of soup, on a tray in front of the TV, with an hour of Magnum, P.I. for dessert. But first, a shower, as much to slough off the lingering odour of hospital antiseptic as to shed the grime of the working day.

The pulsating water soothed and relaxed her, easing away the knotted tension in her neck and shoulders, and sluicing the length of her body like warm, caressing fingers. Stepping out of the tub, she patted herself dry with a thick, velvety towel and finished by massaging herself all over with her favourite body lotion, working the creamy substance into every available inch until her skin gleamed with the soft lustre of a pearl.

She had donned a long blue nightgown of finely ruched silk, and covered it with a flowing caftan of a slightly darker shade when the doorbell rang. Irritated at the intrusion, she shoved her feet into furry white mules and slopped her way to the entrance hall where she squinted at the visitor through the peep-hole.

Diminutively but clearly revealed in the brightly lit hallway outside stood a man in a dark grey bomber jacket, his arms loaded with paper bags, and at the sight of him, Liz recoiled in shock. Con was on one side of her door, casually but fully dressed, and here she was on the other, her hair wrapped, turban-style, in a terry towel and her face devoid of make-up.

Impatiently, the bell sounded again. 'Open the door, Liz, before I drop something. I know you're home.' Con's voice carried clearly, not only to her, but doubtless to every other tenant on the third floor too.

Annoyed, exhilarated, flustered, she released the deadbolt and turned the lock, opening the door to Con, suddenly restored to his normal, larger-than-average size, filling the doorway with his appearance.

'What are you *doing* here?' she demanded, horribly conscious of her shiny nose and the damp strands of hair straggling out of the turban.

'Performing my good deed for the day, ma'am. Aren't you going to ask me in?'

'You hardly waited for an invitation,' she snapped, furious at her body's betrayal, crossing her arms defensively over her breasts and failing completely to still her racing heart. Where was all that steely willpower that had propelled her beyond such girlish flutters?

'The bottom's about to fall out of these bags,' he offered by way of excuse, and unceremoniously dumped one in her arms. 'Lead the way to the kitchen, woman, and stop complaining.'

She opened her mouth to expel a retort blistering enough to stop him in his tracks and found herself, instead, kicking closed the door and following him as he made his way down to the end of the hall and into the kitchen, curiosity and plain, unvarnished, irrepressible pleasure at his sudden arrival erasing her contrived annoyance.

'How did you know I'd be here?'

'You live here. Where else would you be after a hard day in the salt mines?'

'No, I mean, how'd you know I'd be here tonight? You said: "I know you're home".'

'Oh that.' He deposited the bags on the ceramic-tiled counter top and extracted a bottle of wine from the one closest. 'Needs chilling in the freezer for fifteen minutes. How about making me a drink? Scotch and water, no ice.'

Astonished at her own docility, she opened a cupboard to his left, took down a bottle of Chivas Regal, poured a healthy measure into a tumbler and added water. 'You didn't answer my question,' she reminded him, handing over the glass.

'Aren't you going to join me?'

'I'll have a glass of wine later. *Con!*' Exasperation dominated, leaving no room for neurotic apprehension at using his name.

'Ah, a microwave. Great!' Deftly, he stacked cardboard cartons in the oven and set the timer for four minutes. 'Sheila told me. Where are the plates and forks?'

Obediently, she produced the items requested, added paper napkins and wine glasses, then fished out a tray, a move which met with instant approval.

'Good girl. Let's make it casual and cosy, and save the dining room for something more formal. Nice touch, that. You don't often find dining rooms in apartments.'

'When they're as old as this building, you do,' she answered, then dragged her mind back to his earlier remark. 'Sheila? Sheila Johnson?'

'The very same.'

Realising she was gaping slightly, she pressed her lips together for a second before saying more. Sheila, she of the neatly disciplined grey hair and efficient manner who served as receptionist-secretary at the WREN Agency, was not given to the use of Christian names with comparative strangers.

'Great lady,' Con continued. 'Reminds me of home, right down to the chocolate-chip cookies.'

'What are you talking about now?'

'I stopped in the Agency this afternoon, and since you weren't there, Sheila gave me coffee and some of her home-made cookies.'

Perhaps I'm hallucinating, Liz thought. First Susan and the mysterious Mr Chieng; now Con, hobnobbing familiarly with a Sheila turned den mother to an overgrown boy scout.

'Go sit down and put your feet up.' Con's voice broke into her reverie. He was regarding her strangely, scrutinising the exposed features of her face inch by careful inch. 'You look done in. The food's almost ready, and I'll serve.'

Alarm prickled over her skin. She could almost hear the wheels turning in his mind. Dressed as she was, stripped of her sophisticated veneer, she was dangerously affiliated with the banished Willie, and certainly unsuitably attired to receive company.

Hurriedly disappearing into her bedroom, she dragged a comb through the damp tangles of her hair and tamed them to a sort of order, then shed the caftan and gown for a pair of designer jeans and a silk print shirt. About to leave, she turned again to the mirror and touched a soft apricot gloss to her lips.

Not quite as polished an appearance as usual, perhaps, but decidedly Liz. Willie, poor soul, hadn't owned anything with a designer label attached, could barely have squeezed into such sleekly tailored pants, and silk? Heavens above! Polyester was luxury in those long gone days!

She was settled in a corner of the couch when Con appeared with the loaded tray. 'Chinese, okay?'

'So I gathered—and yes, very okay. It beats what I had in mind. Now tell me how you knew I was here and hadn't eaten dinner.'

'I'd like to pass myself off as a super-sensitive mind reader, but it's nothing so exciting.' He was spooning diced almond chicken on to her plate as he spoke, squatting on the edge of the couch and leaning forward so that the short-sleeved knit shirt he wore was stretched taut over his broad shoulders, the corduroy pants clinging to the curve of his thigh. Liz found the whole prospect of him intensely exciting, was intensely aware of the intimacy of the moment.

It was the first time they'd been completely alone since their child was conceived. Did he, she wondered dazedly, her breasts suddenly aching with near-forgotten desire, ever think of that night? Or was it all just a drunken blur, a merciful blank in the life of a young man brought face to face with death for the first time with the arrival of that sad news from Vietnam on his brother, Steve?

'Sheila told me what happened this afternoon. I was still there when you 'phoned her from the hospital, and I figured you'd be pretty wiped out, so . . .' he handed her a steaming plate, huge tiger prawns coated in black bean sauce slivered with ginger, crisp Chinese vegetables and the almond chicken all neatly arranged on chow mein studded with goodies, '. . . I waited till you'd had time to get home, then I 'phoned. I got a busy signal, knew you were here, and stopped by my favourite Chinese takeaway.'

It wasn't a dream, it was perfectly logical, believable reality; good food from the second largest Chinatown in North America, and a man she'd met just a couple of weeks ago to share it with her. The lousy day was going down in a blaze of glory. God, she was happy!

'The wine,' she reminded him, and he leapt up, his long legs unfolding so rapidly he almost upset the low table before them. She called out directions for locating a corkscrew and, while he was gone, rose and went over to the stereo housed in an antique victrola cabinet. Selecting a cassette of Baroque guitar, she plugged in the tape and adjusted the lamps so that the area around the couch was bathed in a pool of soft light.

'Almost perfect.' His voice was deep with hidden undercurrents, and she looked up, startled. She hadn't heard him come back to the living room.

'Almost?' Her breath caught in her throat so that the word was exhaled on a sigh.

He set down the wine, and the glasses he held between the fingers of his other hand. 'A fire,' he murmured. 'To complete the picture. Do you mind?' He held up a lighter, retrieved from the pocket of his trousers.

'Not a bit.'

She always kept a supply of the instant-burning logs that came wrapped in a waxed cover with a guarantee to produce three hours of technicoloured flames. The time was exaggerated, but not so the colours. In a matter of moments, tongues of fire were licking around the wood in blue-green and orange perfection.

'Eat!' he ordered, pouring wine for them both before seating himself close enough beside her that his knee almost touched hers. Surprisingly, she found she was famished and attacked her food with energy.

For a while, conversation lapsed until the edge was off their appetites, then: 'What have you been up to since we had lunch together—besides rescuing your employees from savage beasts, that is?'

'That was a nasty cut Susan got,' she replied severely, reminded by his question of the time that had elapsed since they were together.

'I'm sure it was,' he returned mildly. Glancing up, he caught her examining him and seemed to read the censure in her eyes. 'Why are you upset with me?'

'I'm not,' she answered, too quickly. She smiled brightly, anxious not to have her pleasure in the evening spoiled. He was here now, and that's what counted. She didn't want to remember how she'd been affected by his long silence after their last time together.

'I've been away for nearly two weeks,' he informed her divining her thoughts with devastating accuracy. 'I only got back to town today.'

His words were the antidote to the resentment half formed at the back of her mind. 'You have? Where?'

'In Tokyo for ten days of meetings then up in

northern BC to one of our camps. We have labour
problems developing which I'd like to defuse if I can.'
He speared a prawn and chewed it, eyeing her as he did
so. 'I tried to call you the evening before I left, but you
weren't home—that must have been the Friday after we
were at Verezanno's.'

'The Friday?' Casting her mind back, she remembered
attending the opening of an exhibition by a local artist.
It had been a dreary evening made worse by her longing
to be with Con instead of Jens.

'I was sorry to have missed you.' He selected another
prawn, but this time, a spot of sauce dropped from his
fork and landed on his corduroy-covered thigh.

Without thinking, she reached out a finger to scoop
up the mess, and found herself trembling at the contact
with the rock-hard muscle beneath her fingertip.
Withdrawing her hand, she fumbled blindly with the
other to find her napkin, wondering what in the world
had prompted her to make such an intimate gesture.

The napkin wasn't there. It had slid from her lap to
the floor, but even as she searched for it, he solved the
difficulty. His hand, well-shaped and lightly tanned,
clasped her about the wrist and drew her towards him.

She raised startled eyes and found herself impaled by
the blue intensity of his gaze as, slowly but inexorably,
he pulled her hand to his mouth and took her extended
fingertip between his lips in a gesture so blatantly erotic
that a hot tide of passion swept up her body and
engulfed her. Slowly and with excruciating deliberation,
his tongue explored the sensitive tip, acquainting itself
with the delicate cuticle, the smooth oval nail and
finally, agonisingly, travelling the length of her finger
and coming to rest in the palm of her hand.

It was the most profoundly moving experience of her
life, touching something deep and elemental within her
that not even the ill-fated passion of their youth had
awoken. For just a moment or two, time hung
suspended and trapped her in ecstasy.

The pressure on her wrist increased. Like a

sleepwalker, her eyelids heavy, her vision clouded, she watched as he lifted his head, his gaze never once leaving her face, and touched his lips to hers. All the pent-up longings of a lifetime surged through her, a reservoir of blighted hopes and unfulfilled dreams fighting for release, for rebirth. Those lips, speaking a language of love without uttering a single word, the same lips that had led her from innocence to knowledge, from ignorance to gnawing hunger.

Briefly, she melted against him, before caution reared up and her sense of self-preservation, honed by long years of service, cut through the moment with the swiftness of a tempered blade.

'No ... no ... please.' She attempted to pull back, her voice weak and disembodied, but Con merely raised his other hand, the one that had come to rest along the back of the couch, and cupped it behind her head, drawing her more firmly to him. Every sense enlivened to the danger of surrendering—again—to the one man capable of levelling her resistance, she pressed both palms flat against his chest, panic giving impetus to her actions.

Reluctantly, he lifted his head, a query plain in his eyes. Something had happened—surely not a mere kiss?—yet something had drawn that curtain of reserve around her, veiling her in secrecy, only the dying flush on her cheeks testifying to her brief surrender. 'Liz?'

'I'm sorry. I'm not ... comfortable with the situation.'

He scarcely believed his ears. He almost laughed. And yet, behind the controlled façade, there lurked an impression of ... pain.

He released her gently and leaned back, then took her hand again and held it carefully. It fluttered in his grasp like a wounded bird. 'It's all right,' he told her. 'I won't rush you. You don't have to do anything you're not ready for.'

Gradually his voice calmed the hidden terror, freed her from the past and brought her back to the present.

'I know it's fashionable,' she began, 'to . . . jump into . . . involvements. It's just that, for me, it isn't right. We hardly . . .'

'Know each other,' he finished for her. It was exactly what she'd been about to say, until the irony of the words struck her.

'More or less,' she agreed.

'Then let me change your mind,' he murmured, 'because I feel I've known you—been waiting for you all my life.'

Realeasing her hand, he cupped her face, his thumbs tracing the high angle of her cheekbones. 'These lips were made to be kissed,' he whispered, and lowered his mouth once more to hers, not with fiery, frightening passion but with a gentleness far more brutal, for it rendered her incapable of resistance.

Like a blind man confronted with the unknown, he explored the soft fullness, the sweet curve of her mouth, his tongue probing yet delicately attuned to her needs. There was no need to force, to persuade. Her lips opened as petals before the sun and welcomed his warmth, blooming with a passion he accepted with grateful reverence.

Something primitive and long suppressed stirred and quivered, thrusting upwards through the layers of self-protective reserve, erupting into a moan of reluctant ecstasy deep in her throat. Her hands slid up the broad chest, snaked around his neck and urged him fiercely closer.

It was the response he'd waited for. With an answering murmur, he gathered her hungrily to him, his tongue suddenly demanding, his hands weaving unspeakable magic as they charted the hitherto forbidden territory of her body through the thin silk of her shirt, then trespassing inside the loose neckline, invading the shadowed cleft between her breasts, tracing fleetingly over the silken upper curves before brushing the full undersides with his palm.

His hair, so thick and unruly, seemed to entrap her

restless fingers, his mouth branding her everywhere it touched—her eyelids, her earlobes, the hidden hollows of her collarbones. 'Let me love you,' he urged, his voice hoarse with desire.

Let me, let me! The same words, the same voice, more frenzied, less resonant, echoed down the years, triggering alarm bells that clanged with strident insistence.

'NO!' Her voice emerged high-pitched with panic.

'What?' He raised molten blue eyes to hers, bewildered. 'Trust me. I want to get to know you, lovely Liz. I want to know all about you.'

Hope flared briefly before apprehension ran clammy fingers down her spine. He must not, *could* not, be allowed to come too close.

'Liz?'

She jumped at the sound of his voice, so near, so warm. 'Yes?'

'I said, I want to——'

'I know. I heard you.'

'But?'

She pushed feebly at his chest, the gesture ineffectual in dampening either his ardour or his persistence. 'Nothing,' she murmured. 'Just stop.'

'That's all you have to say?'

It was not a good time to play cat-and-mouse games with him. It had been too long and frustrating and, finally, too shattering a day, and she was not at her most alert. It would be too easy to get herself trapped into incriminating revelation; *much* too easy to let herself fall under his spell again.

'I'm really very tired,' she announced baldly. 'I appreciate your stopping by with dinner. It was delicious. But I'd like to call it a day.'

'I can take a hint,' he returned drily, 'even one as subtle as that.'

They rose together and he retrieved his jacket from the kitchen, then came to where she stood in the hall, her hand pointedly on the door, ready to spur him to a speedy exit.

'But,' he continued, unmoved by her impatience to see him gone, 'I don't discourage easily. I intend to follow through on what I said earlier: I *do* want to get to know you. There's something between us—I can't explain it—and you haven't seen the last of me.' His head dipped down and before she had time to guess his intention, he brought his lips to hers in a brief hard kiss.

Traffic was heavy as late-night shoppers joined the crowds streaming from the early shows at the cinemas. Easing the dark blue Cadillac Seville into the stream of cars heading towards the Lions Gate Bridge and the north shore of the city, Con mulled over the last couple of hours.

He was enormously drawn to her, but she seemed determined to hold him off. Yet, he could swear she was just as attracted to him as he was to her. He was far too experienced not to recognise the signs, and, he liked to think, sensitive enough not to force his attentions on someone unwilling to accept them.

She was sending out contradictory signals. How could he reconcile the closed look on her face, the cool verbal dismissal, with the yearning angle of her body when he kissed her, the soft eager lips beneath his?

She must be in her late twenties, he judged, not only because of her professional status but because she possessed that air of calm certainty that only came from maturity. He couldn't believe he was the first man to pursue her. He couldn't accept that she was afraid or totally inexperienced. With her attributes, she must have a flock of guys angling for her.

Swinging into the centre lane on the approach to the bridge, he compressed his lips and a small muscle twitched in his jaw. It didn't really matter who or how many had tried before him; from now on, he intended to decimate the opposition.

At eleven o'clock, Liz flung back the covers, climbed

out of bed and, opening the curtains, gazed out at the night scene spread below her, a scene at once so frenziedly urban yet so majestically untamed by human hand. To the south, an unceasing stream of traffic flashed headlights in hypnotic sequence between the iron supports of the Burrard Street Bridge. To the west and north, the mountains loomed, remote and black against an indigo sky.

And superimposing on it all, Con's image, tantalising and forbidden. How well she could recall every last detail of his face. He *had* changed over the years. Tonight, she'd noticed the glint of silver in his hair, the marks of disillusionment on his face. He was definitely older, looked every one of his thirty-five years, but had lost none of his magnetism because of it. If anything, he was even more attractive, more compelling, than the young man she'd known before.

And that, right there, was the best possible reason for ending this relationship before it began, because heaven knew how impossible he'd been to resist before. Remembering was painful enough; she really didn't need to refresh her memory by exposing herself to new hurts.

It's really quite simple, she told herself. Don't play with fire and you won't get burned. You're lucky you're able to recognise the danger.

So rational, so safe. So why was she standing there, shivering from the cold and something else not so easily defined? Why did she feel so bereft, as though she'd just been robbed of something precious?

'I want to know all about you,' he'd said.

Did he really? Did he want to know that she was the girl who'd given herself so wholly to him the night he'd heard about his brother's death; the girl to whom he'd never, not once during that long, wonderful, terrible night, referred by name, probably because he didn't know who she was and cared even less? Did he really want to learn that what had been, to him, a buffer for his pain, much like the rye he'd consumed with such ferocious intent, had been to her the single most important event in her life?

For a few short hours, all the trite silly sayings had come true: she *was* walking on air, her head in the clouds. She'd believed she'd been given something unique and precious. How naïve she'd been then, poor dumb Willie. But she'd learned and she'd changed.

The trouble was, so had he. He was older and smarter. He knew his earlier technique of persuasive fumbling wasn't enough. Silly little girls might shed their clothes with a sad disregard for all they'd been taught, but not sophisticated women of thirty. Even in this day of sexual freedom, he wouldn't expect her to be an easy conquest. He'd be prepared to woo her, but the end result would be the same. He'd seduce her, enslave her, and move on to new challenges. And she'd be right back where she'd started, twelve years ago—without the added complication of a pregnancy, of course. That was the one thing she'd never again have to worry about. That was, perhaps, the saddest realisation of all.

It was clear where she had to go from here. She must never again spend time alone with Con. Addicts could remain whole and functioning as long as they avoided their addictive habits. *She* could survive, but not if she subjected herself to the powerful effect of Con's sensual assault. Her obsession with him would destroy her.

CHAPTER FOUR

GOOD intentions were a marvellous thing, sustaining her until almost ten o'clock the next morning, when the 'phone jarred her from the comforting folds of sleep. She extended one arm from under the covers to fumble for the offending instrument, snarling the cord around her wrist in concertina coils as she drew the receiver into the haven of warmth created by the duvet.

'Hello?' Her croak of greeting would have rivalled a toad's.

'Good morning.' Con's voice was a muted growl of seduction in her ear, bringing her fully awake and alert to the danger of him. 'Did I disturb you?'

'Yes,' she answered shortly. 'Weekends are my only chance to sleep in and I rather enjoy that.'

'Then I'm sorry I called so soon, but I was afraid, if I left it too long, you might make other plans for tonight.'

'Tonight? What about tonight?'

'I'd like to take you out to dinner—something more exotic than last night's picnic.'

A pause lengthened into embarrassing silence as she searched for some succinct way to convey her absolute uninterest in furthering the relationship.

'Liz?'

'I'm here.' Mental agility was not her strong point before the first cup of coffee of the day. Add to that the lurch of sensual delight that ran rampant through her veins at the sound of his voice, and articulating the simplest response became a major undertaking.

'I'm bowled over at your enthusiasm.'

'I'm busy tonight.'

'Uh-huh. With me, I hope.'

'Not with you. I have other plans.'

'Cancel them. Tell whoever he is I'm your long lost lover come back to claim you.'

'That's not funny,' she protested sharply, stabbed by the careless accuracy of his words.

'And I'm not joking.' He almost purred, but there was steel under the velvet. 'I'd really like to see you tonight.'

'I'll be out.'

'Perhaps later then? We'll postpone dinner for another time.'

The desire to yield fought a brief and bitter battle with the will to survive, the victory of head over heart affording her not the slightest gratification. 'That's not a good idea.'

'At least consider it, and call me if you change your mind.' He recited a telephone number which she made no effort to record.

'I doubt I'll do that.'

'We'll see.' He hung up gently and left her vibrating with agitation. New-born resolve faltered with the temptation to gamble with love. If only she dared to explore a relationship with Con . . .

Tossing back the covers, she slid from the bed, knowing that positive, organised action was the best antidote to the uncertainty that was taking hold of her. Pulling a fleece jogging suit from the closet, she marched doggedly through to the bathroom, grimly determined to enjoy a reviving run along the sea-wall. It was either that or burrowing back into a cocoon of quilted comfort and hoping what afflicted her would go away like the 'flu.

It was a brisk, windy day, the sailboats dipping and weaving in a sort of mating dance around the freighters lying at anchor off English Bay. Great marshmallow clouds ballooned over the near hills and shrouded the mountain tops, but the sun was shining as she set off along Pacific Avenue, past the covered band-shell, and down on to the seawall into Stanley Park.

She would never become immune to the view, she

decided, settling into stride and inhaling the sharp, salty air, her spirits rising despite Con. Vine maples were a riot of glorious red, beeches and alder vivid yellow, and she was immensely cheered by the pleasure she was able to take in her surroundings. It showed that, absorbing and disruptive though she found him, Con had not acquired his earlier stranglehold on her emotions.

When she returned to the apartment building two hours later, soaked to the skin from the sudden downpour of rain that had blown in from the ocean, there was a florist's box at her door and her 'phone was ringing.

'Yes?' She was breathless, dripping rainwater on the oiled perfection of the oak floor, the florist's box was too large to set down on the table, and her tone was anything but gracious. 'Hello?' She spoke again, erasing the edge of irritation from her voice, annoyed with herself for allowing such petty details to rattle her.

'It's Jens, Liz. I tried calling you earlier, but you must have been out.'

Very good, Jens. Go to the top of the class. 'I just got in. How are you, Jens?'

Curious, she slid the ribbon from the box and lifted the lid to take a peek at the contents, The scent of carnations, masses of them in a lovely soft shade of apricot, wrapped her about in spicy perfume.

'Great. I just wanted to settle on a time for tonight. How about if I stop by for you around seven, seven-thirty?'

'Tonight?' she echoed abstractedly, poking among the tissue paper for the card located somewhere in the profusion of flowers.

'Yes, the Haywood party. You hadn't forgotten, had you?'

Of course she'd forgotten. Since the advent of Con Henderson into her life, she seemed incapable of operating on all cylinders. But what a fortuitous reminder! She hadn't lied to Con after all.

'Oh, Jens,' she murmured, lifting one delicate bloom

and caressing her cheek with it, 'of course I hadn't forgotten. I'm looking forward to it.' Maybe if she sounded sincere enough, she'd convince herself. 'There's just one thing . . .'

'What's that?'

'Can we stop somewhere first for a bite to eat? Just a snack or something? The last time we were at the Haywoods', they served a very late buffet. I thought I'd faint from hunger, and I don't care to fill up on all those fattening nibblies they offer.'

The fact was, she didn't entirely trust Con not to show up, despite her refusal to have dinner with him. An even sadder fact was that, if he did, she wasn't at all sure she'd be able to hold out against that fatal charm of his.

'You don't need to worry about your weight.' Jens was predictably gallant, predictably . . . predictable. 'But sure, I'll pick you up around six-thirty and we'll stop for quiche or something first.'

Real men don't eat quiche! The uncharitable thought blazed across her mind before she could contain it. 'Lovely,' she murmured, ashamed of her hypocrisy. 'See you then.'

Oh honestly! Jens had been a perfectly pleasant, perfectly acceptable escort until Con had shown up. She was in perfect control with Jens. Now, his niceness, the safety she felt with him, were falling away and leaving him looking somehow ridiculous, as though he'd been caught in public wearing droopy boxer shorts.

Cradling the flowers in her arms, she paddled through to the kitchen, leaving a pattern of wet prints behind her. Depositing the box on the counter, she went through to the bathroom and turned on the shower, emerging fifteen minutes later feeling slightly more kindly disposed to the world.

A vase, she decided, pulling the belt on her terry-cloth robe snugly around her waist; perhaps two or three, in fact. There were at least six dozen carnations waiting for her attention.

Almost reluctantly, she picked up the small white
envelope and extracted the card from inside. How like
him his writing is, she thought, surveying the message
inscribed in a firm, confident hand on the folded scrap
of paper.

She'd known all along the flowers were from Con.
Who else was given to such extravagance? Not Jens,
who sent a dozen long-stemmed roses every other
month or so, but who lacked the flamboyance to buy
out the florist's entire stock.

A wave of forbidden pleasure washed over her as she
searched out containers and set about arranging the
flowers. When she'd finished, they lit up the apartment
with their warm glow, breathing life and colour into the
drab overcast of the day.

Furtively, as if someone might be watching, she
placed the card in a hidden drawer in her jewellery box
and chose to ignore the reasons for her whimsical
behaviour. The message lay hidden, but not forgotten.
'Every once in a while, someone like you comes along
and someone like me gets lucky. Con.'

The evening with Jens was an unqualified disaster
from the outset. The dreary hours stretched into
forever, and, as a grand finale, Jens chose the
occasion to flex his seductive muscles as it were,
abandoning his hitherto faultlessly correct overtures
and going so far, on the drive home, as to lay a
possessive hand on her knee and let his fingers stray
under the hem of her dress, in search of her silk-clad
thigh. Her vigorous swat to his wrist, delivered in
tandem with a frigidly repressive glare, rendered him
speechless with embarrassment, while his efforts to
remove the offending fingers inconspicuoulsy rendered
him ridiculous. Dismissing him outside the building
without even permitting him to escort her inside to
her door was the ultimate blow, and he slunk away
into the night, a seemingly defeated man.

So much for Jens! Liz concluded, as she left the

wrought-iron elegance of the lift and made her way to her own front door. If Con disposes of the rest of my friends with equal dispatch, I may *have* to turn to him for companionship.

Her key was in the lock when the bitter-sweet object of her thoughts rose up from the sill of the window embrasure at the end of the hall. The movement caught Liz's eye and she watched with fearful fascination as Con covered the distance between them in three long strides.

He was the picture of masculine refinement, his white silk shirt in pristine contrast to the dark blue suit he wore. Liz swallowed, her throat dry and an actual pain piercing the region of her heart at the sheer male beauty of him. He's all dressed up, was her unreasonable reaction. He went out without me!

He was the first to speak. Shooting back his cuff, he took marked note of the time on the gold Rolex, then regarded her from under raised brows. 'It is now, by my reckoning, exactly twenty-one minutes after twelve, an unhealthy hour for a lady to be out alone. I hope you don't make a habit of it. Give me your key.'

Dumbfounded at his impudence, she stood back and allowed him to precede her into her apartment, where he stood like an attendant executioner, holding open the door.

'Let's not wast any more of this evening,' he urged her softly.

It was the nervous fluttering in her stomach that brought her to her senses. Why was she feeling so guilty? This was *her* apartment, *her* life, and if he'd wasted his time hanging around for her, he had only himself to blame.

'My evening wasn't wasted, Con,' she remarked calmly. 'And I'm sorry if yours was. Why are you here?'

'In answer to the 'phone call you were going to make the minute you came in.'

'But I wasn't planning to call you. I was planning on going to bed.'

'Hallelujah!' He favoured her with a comically lewd wink.

'Alone—so keep a tight rein on your unholy lust!' She walked past and away from him. It was one thing to rattle off verbal sallies, quite another to look at him as she did so.

The scent of carnations assailed her, and she hesitated before continuing, 'The flowers are lovely. Thank you.'

He closed the door with a soft thud and followed her into the living room, standing before the fireplace with his hands thrust into the hip pockets of his trousers, his unbuttoned jacket revealing the fine tailoring of the suit, and the sleek, masculine lines of the body beneath it.

Wrenching her gaze away from his long legs straddled in front of the hearth in dark contrast to the pale decor, she turned and dropped her coat over the back of a chair. 'Thanks also for seeing me inside the door. Now that you know I'm home safe, you can leave with a clear conscience.'

'Spend tomorrow with me.'

Oh God, he was going to prolong the agony. 'No.'

'Why not?'

'I can't, that's all.'

'Can't, or won't?'

'Can't,' she replied truthfully. Would that she could! But that way led to the destruction of all she'd striven for. Just the brief encounters of the last weeks illustrated how disastrously he could undermine her proud strength with a mere glance.

'Monday evening, then.'

'No.'

'Tuesday, Wednesday—name the night.'

A sudden rush of tears pricked her vision—tears for the too-late arrival of words she'd once longed to hear from him. 'No!' She barely managed to keep her voice steady.

'Are you telling me you're not interested in seeing me

again? That you don't feel the current that's running between us, right now, at this very minute?'

'Exactly.' It was a whisper hounded by despair.

His voice, which had been frayed with irritation, was suddenly smooth as cream and disturbingly close behind her. 'Liar,' he crooned, shifting the fabric of her dress so that he could plant a lingering kiss where the curve of her shoulder disappeared below the wide neckline. Dizziness assailed her, dimming her vision and churning her blood, and she reached for the table in front of her.

'Liar,' he repeated, the husky edge to his voice betraying his own arousal, his lips trailing with fatal tenderness up the side of her neck and coming to rest at her ear. 'Tell me to my face that you don't want to see me again.'

His hands spanned the narrowness of her waist, and spun her gently around, holding her immovably against him, the contact of his thighs against hers sapping her of the power to stand unaided. Fractionally, she leaned into his chest, her lips apart as she gasped for the strength to rebuff him. 'I don't ...' she began, then made the mistake of raising her eyes to his, '... don't ... want ...' The words faltered to a stop, evaporating in the heated intensity of his gaze.

'You do,' he contradicted her softly. 'You want, just as much as I want.'

Her instinct for survival swirled and melted in the cobalt depths of his eyes, demolished by the sensuous shadow of his lashes as they swept low in an effort to bank the fires of his own passion. His closeness, his breath winnowing over her face, the clean, manly scent of him assaulted her like a powerful narcotic, leaving her helpless to deny him.

Lowering her own bronze-tipped lashes, she fought to hide her response, but he felt it in the fine tremor that shook her, read it in the sultry droop of her mouth. Where moments earlier she had been all brittle, angular hostility, she was now soft, yielding warmth.

'Don't fight me, Liz.' His lips were mere inches from hers, and moving closer. 'It's a battle I'll never let you win.'

He sealed the threat by touching his lips to her face with unswerving determination. Expertly, mercilessly, he stripped away the layers of her reserve and scattered her fears; gently, relentlessly, he led her out of the drought of her self-denial, his kisses cascading over her eyes, her nose, her cheeks and settling at last on lips that had grown restive and hungry for his.

It was so ineffably *right* that, when his tongue teased the contours of her mouth, she should permit it entry, and not the least bit untoward that she should welcome its searching forays. It was impossible to remain impassive beneath his tender exploration; unnatural not to respond, not to savour the taste and texture of him with the same thorough appreciation he extended to her. When his lips slid away to trace a fragile path down the slender arch of her neck, a whimper of loss escaped her, subsiding into a moan of pure delight as his mouth, moist and eager, settled on her pulsing throat.

Hands that had risen to repel, slipped in fluid curves around his neck, cradling his head close as though to capture forever the source of the tiny, tender kisses that followed the outline of her collarbone. And all the time, *his* hands, the long fingers splayed over the soft flare of her buttocks, held her in a close, revealing welding of hip and thigh.

He knew he had levelled the barriers she'd erected so painstakingly. When he slipped an arm around her shoulders, another behind her knees, and lifted her to him, she melted into his hold, and rested parted lips below his ear, the fingers of one hand threaded through his hair, those of the other timidly venturing inside his shirt. The glance he turned on her seared her, mesmerised her, drained her of the capacity to reason, and left her hollow with hunger for more . . . and closer . . .

One of her sling-back sandals, a strappy, soft grey suede creation with a narrow, spiked heel, fell unheeded to the rug as he turned from the living room into the hallway leading to the bedroom. Her hair, earlier pinned into a cluster of curls, spilled free and lay in fine strands of pale and shining bronze on the dark blue fabric of his suit.

In one smooth motion, he laid her on the bed and shrugged out of his jacket, loosening his tie and unbuttoning the cuffs of his shirt. Throughout it all, his gaze devoured her, never once leaving her face, as though he hardly dared believe the surrender he read in her eyes, her eagerness in her trembling mouth.

Swiftly, he came to sit beside her, his hands reaching behind to undo her dress and push it aside to reveal her bared shoulders, the lacy nonsense of her bra. Trailing fire and throbbing turmoil in their wake, his thumbs feathered up her ribs and, with the utmost delicacy, toured the gentle swell of her breasts.

'I can't believe how exquisite you are,' he whispered and brought his head down to nestle reverent lips at the base of her throat, just below the frenzied fluttering pulse, just above the aching, straining flesh that yearned to be free of constraint and at the mercy of his touch.

Liz didn't know how long the doorbell had been ringing before it penetrated the outer rim of their absorption with each other, but when, finally, it impinged on her conscious mind, she came instantly to the shocked realisation that she was half naked and that the skirt of her dress had ridden up to expose an indecent length of thigh.

'Ignore it,' Con begged, stopping her hand from straightening the disarray, and savouring the honey of her skin with renewed intensity. Whether he referred to her attempts to cover herself, or the persistent clamour of the bell, wasn't quite clear. Nor did it matter. The moment, which had been as ethereal as spun glass, shattered into a million pieces.

'I can't——' she protested, her breath surging in

uneven gasps. She was immeasurably distressed, and far too confused to know why this was so. Only much later, in her self-imposed loneliness, would she wonder: was it his successful seduction—or the fact that it was incomplete?

'It's nothing . . . important.' He ran his hands up and covered her ears, shutting out the intrusive din.

'It *might* be.'

With a sudden twist, she was on the other side of the bed from him, and on her feet in a flash, pulling her clothing to rights with fingers that shook. 'I *have* to see who it is—at this hour.'

It was not yet one o'clock. How could so much have taken place, in such a short time?

The bell sounded again, twice. She opened the door and came face to face with Jens, his finger poised to ring until he received an answer.

'Liz! I had to come back. I couldn't leave things the way they were.' His forehead was ridged with unhappiness, his whole demeanour despondent. 'When you didn't answer, I began to worry. I didn't wake you, did I?'

The question seemed to draw immediate attention to her appearance, and she was blushingly aware of her dishevelled condition. He saw it, too. The slump melted out of his shoulders as he drew himself stiffly erect, the chill blue of his Scandinavian eyes glazing with the realisation of what her swollen mouth and flushed cheeks denoted.

It was like the first time Con had made love to her and she'd had to face her mother. Shame swept over her in great waves and her gaze fell to the foot or so of floor that separated them. 'No, you didn't wake me.' Her reply was barely audible.

'Obviously not,' he replied in a clipped tone, and venturing an upward glance at his stern features, she saw that he'd noticed her sandal sprawled wantonly on its side in gaping indecency. Somehow, it made her feel more exposed than if she'd come to answer his summons naked. Indeed, the frozen disapproval of his gaze shot terror through her as she wondered if, in her haste, she *was* revealing more of herself than she'd realised.

Furtively, she brought her arms up to cover breasts that still throbbed faintly from the onslaught of Con's skilled lips, but the gesture did not go unnoticed and a grimace marred Jens' handsome features.

Inexplicably, she apologised. 'I'm sorry, Jens.'

'Are you?' he asked, his gaze shooting over her shoulder to something behind her that provoked his even greater displeasure.

'No need to apologise, my love.' Con's voice electrified her momentarily, then she swivelled around to find him lounging in the open doorway leading to the bedroom, his shirt unbuttoned and hanging outside the waist of his trousers. His feet were bare, and his hair— surely it hadn't been that tousled before? He was the very picture of a man about to take his woman to bed, and Jens' pinched nostrils and hissing intake of breath made it only too clear the same thought had occurred to him, and that he was fully aware of which woman that would be.

'It would seem I should be the one to apologise.' Jens' words were frosted with disapproval at all he witnessed. 'Obviously, I have interrupted ... *something*.'

The last word gusted forth with an air of such distaste that Liz was washed anew with shame, but Con, strolling forward and draping a familiar arm around her shoulders, let out a bellow of mirth.

'You could say that,' he chortled, 'but we've got all night to make up for it.' The laughter dwindled abruptly and he fixed Jens with his electric blue stare. 'Provided, of course, you've finished what you came to say. There *wasn't* anything more, was there?'

'Nothing at all.' With a stiff nod in their general direction, Jens wheeled about and marched down the hall to the lift, and Con reached forward a negligent foot and kicked closed the door.

'Where were we?' he enquired, preparing to draw her into his arms.

'We weren't anywhere,' Liz was bristling with anger and embarrassment. 'You can get dressed and follow him.'

'What?' He pretended innocent surprise, but the crinkly laugh lines at the corners of his eyes betrayed his ill concealed mirth. 'What's the matter, Liz? Surely you're not letting *him* upset you?' He dismissed Jens with a contemptuous toss of his head.

'He's not upsetting me, you are. How *could* you appear like that and say those awful things?'

'Awful things? What awful things? I was telling the truth, and they didn't seem to strike you as so very awful before what's-his-name showed up. In fact,' he drawled, tracing an impudent finger over her breast, and smiling into her eyes, 'you seemed to be enjoying them as much as I was.'

To her chagrin, his touch inflamed her, rousing the sensitive nipple into jutting life, a response of which he was instantly aware.

'See?' he taunted her softly, and cupped the betraying breast in his palm. 'Don't be angry, sweetheart. It's a waste of energy. Come back to bed and let me love you.'

Just briefly, she wavered, and Con, sensing this, pulled her to him, cradling her head against his shoulder. 'Come back to me,' he whispered. 'Forget the Jolly Blond Giant.'

The unfortunate remark was Con's undoing. Pushing away from him with surprising energy, she broke free of his hold, her humiliation at the recent confrontation with Jens flooding over her with fresh force. Where was her self-respect? She'd known Jens for months and not once, in all that time, had she ever had reason to cringe at her conduct—until tonight. And just like old times, she'd allowed Con—again—to persuade her to ignore her better judgment, and for what? So that, hot on the heels of her prudish reaction to Jens' tentative overtures, she could, in the space of half an hour, prove to him what a hypocritical trollop she really was.

Twelve years of practise wasn't time enough, after all, for Liz Newman to learn how to play the game. In one evening, she'd damn near fallen into bed with the one man whose bewitching charm could annihilate her, and ruined her carefully preserved image with Jens.

'This probably means nothing to you,' she declared bitingly, 'but Jens happens to be an old and valued friend of mine. You've already done your best to drive him away. Please don't add to things by insulting him behind his back.'

'I see.' Con slipped his hands into his side pockets and regarded her from under lowered brows. 'What, then, happened earlier that this "old and valued friend" felt the need to come and display such abject remorse?'

'That's none of your business.'

He aimed a dazzling grin at her, then straightened his features into a caricature of Puritan dismay. 'He made a pass at you, didn't he? The bounder! The cad! He tried to *lay hands on your body beautiful*!'

'Shut up!' She spat the words at him.

'Shut up? Tsk, tsk, Elizabeth. Such unseemly language for a lady. No wonder Blondie was hard pressed to act the gentleman.'

'You wouldn't know a gentleman if you fell over one,' she retorted, furious at him and at herself for letting him shatter her composure. 'You *would* assume Jens has the morals of an alley cat—it's the only sort of behaviour you understand.'

The grin was inching back, beginning with a dimple to the right of his mouth. The blue eyes danced with laughter and that hair, so alive with shining vitality, seemed charged with its own form of amusement as it sprang in unruly disorder across his forehead.

'Honey,' he infirmed her, his words rippling with glee, '*any* guy who's been around you long enough to be regarded as an "old and valued friend" and who hasn't choked on the title is afflicted with serious problems.'

Real men don't eat quiche! There it was again, that snide, destructive notion, insinuating itself to the forefront of her mind. 'Go away,' she said wearily. 'Just leave me alone. I don't want to listen to any more of this. Hearing your words makes me feel ... dirty. Women are just objects to you, things to be used for your own gratification.'

She'd finally pierced his little bubble of fun. The grin was wiped off his face, to be replaced by an expression of shocked surprise.

'You know that's not what's going on here,' he insisted. 'I admit, I appreciate a beautiful woman as much as the next guy, and you'll know I'm dead the day I don't, but what's happening between you and me isn't just a matter of appetite.'

'Call it what you like,' she responded listlessly. 'It all boils down to the same thing: you want to get me into bed and you don't care how you do it or who gets hurt.'

'Oh grow up, Liz.' For the first time, there was impatience in his tone. 'This isn't the last century, and you're not a child. There's absolutely nothing "dirty" about my desire for you, and you're a fool if you think physical love is nothing more than unbridled lust. Do you really equate what we could have with that disgraceful occurrence between your employees and mine a few weeks back?'

Did she? Had she become so soured that she reduced everything between a man and a woman to the lowest level? Didn't she believe in romantic love any longer?

'Well?'

'I don't know. Right now, I don't care. I just want to be alone.' She sounded like a goddess of the silver screen, but inside, she felt like a child afraid of the dark. 'Please ...' She gestured towards the door and was miserably rewarded by Con's shrug of acceptance.

'Okay, if that's how you want to play it. But——' he stopped *en route* to the bedroom to retrieve his jacket and shoes, '—it doesn't end here. If it's time you need, I can accept that and I'll be as patient as I know how.

What I absolutely will not do is let you walk away and pretend we've never met.'

Shrugging into his jacket, he strolled over to where she stood by the front door, and reached out an indolent finger to tilt up her chin. Too proud to glance away, too cowardly to meet his gaze head on, she compromised by staring intently at his left ear. 'This is the second night in a row you've kicked me out,' he observed mildly. 'Don't let it become a habit.'

Disappointingly, he left without so much as a kiss.

She wanted to feel his arms around her, to thrill to the touch of his lips in places no one else's had ever touched. Would he believe she had experienced a man's lovemaking only once in her life, when she was still in her teens? Would he believe he was that man?

Hardly. She was an anachronism, a slightly shopsoiled virgin of thirty, untutored and unsure, yet lacking that intact innocence that might have lent her a unique appeal.

And what did Con really want? His words sounded so fine, so reasonable. Even knowing how cavalier he'd been before, she was tempted to trust him, until she went over the evening together again and realised he'd really promised her nothing. Certainly, he found her attractive, and he'd made it more than clear that he'd be willing to engage in an affair, but what then? Considering the shape she'd been in after his first rejection, how would she handle it a second time?

And yet, it was he, tonight, who'd chided her for cheapening what lay between them, leaving her still to answer her own unspoken question: didn't she believe in love any more? Was it all just an exercise in sexual warfare to her?

If so, why had it been so crucial that she make herself over as attractively as possible? Of course, the packaging camouflaged the incomplete woman inside, but there was, she admitted with uneasy reluctance, another reason.

The truth was, she'd thirsted for romantic love and

done her level best to be its worthy recipient. And when opportunity had presented itself in the tentative shape of Jens and a half dozen clones with equal potential for satisfying this driving need, she'd found that man plus woman did not equal magic. Chemistry was neither to be acquired nor imitated.

Still, she'd nursed a secret hope, barely acknowledged even to herself, that some time, someone would come along who would displace Con in her heart. Oh, not with the same rush of grand passion, perhaps. Only the very young or the very fortunate were granted that, it seemed. But, despite her best intentions, she remained untouched, unmoved by any stirrings of desire.

In a way, it had been a useful discovery, for it had precluded any need for her to explain her sterility or its cause. One did not, concluded the cool, distant Ms Newman, disclose one's most private and painful secrets to a consort for whom one experienced only the most tepid affection.

Her seeming frigidity towards men having been established and accepted, she'd foolishly believed herself cured of her youthful infatuation. She found herself, now, impotently enraged at this latest, most distressing betrayal of her wayward heart. For, while *in absentia*, it was easy to blame Con for her present neuroses, in the flesh he simply refused to live down to her expectations of him as a manipulator and user, selfish and indifferent to others. Try though she might to pin darkly suspect motives to his behaviour, he confounded her at every turn, not once adopting the role for which she'd believed him so suitably cast.

For her, there was, still, would always be, Con. Despite everything—all the pain and humiliation and loss—he was the only man she'd ever loved, and not all her efforts could free her of this consuming passion. Paradoxically, she was filled with elation and despair. For safety's sake, she must tread warily. He could never be allowed to guess how deeply she cared.

CHAPTER FIVE

NOVEMBER raged in on tattered gales and slashing rain, but in the stores the glitter of Christmas began to appear. Right on cue, the Agency's bookings tripled and Liz was persuaded to hire student help to cope with the seasonal rush.

'Give the kids a break, right?' Janice, book-keeper and general budget minder, was gleeful at the unprecedented flow of business. 'We might even need a couple of permanent full-timers.'

'Let's not rush into that.' Liz remained cautious, unwilling to have to lay off anyone if the January slump followed its normal course. 'Students don't depend on us for a steady income, and they know the work's only temporary.'

'Well, it was just a thought. How long before Susan is back in commission?

'The stitches come out tomorrow, so I'd expect her to be in on Monday.' It had been almost a week since Susan Franks had injured her hand.

'Pity it can't be sooner. We've got a rush of bookings over the next two days.'

'Anything special?'

'Well, nothing we can't handle, but we're going to have to juggle schedules. There's an engagement party out near the university after lunch, and Henderson Industries want someone at their entertainment suite this afternoon instead of tomorrow. There's a big client coming in from the Far East tonight. He's bringing his wife along and they want the works—spit and polish, flowers, magazines, city info—but they'll take care of stocking the bar.'

It had been five days since she'd seen or heard from Con; five nights since his hands and lips had left their scalding imprint on her body. The carnations still glowed against the drab grey outdoors, two of them in a bud vase on her office desk, as vivid as the memories she tried to suppress, yet a powerful hunger for something more gnawed at her.

'Let me help,' she suggested, seizing the opportunity to assuage her craving, safely. Even an impersonal business connection would help, give substance and dimension to the tenuous relationship she shared with Con without undermining her resolve to keep him at arm's length. 'Who's slated to take care of the Henderson job?'

'Nadine Baxter, but she has a dental appointment at four.'

'No problem.' Liz waved an airy hand and ran a finger down her daily planner. 'I've got nothing on after two, so I'll pick up the flowers and magazines and all that stuff, and finish off for her. Tell her I'll be there by three, half-past at the very latest.'

'Sure you want to do this?'

'Why not? It won't be the first time.'

'I know, but you didn't seem too impressed with the big boss that day he showed up here. In fact, I don't think I've ever seen you quite so flustered. You were all set to cancel the contract.'

Liz felt a warm pink suffuse her face, but her voice was cool, brazenly indifferent, as she replied, 'Oh, we sorted all that out.'

'*Did* you?'

She glanced up to find Janice's speculative gaze taking interested note of her reactions. 'Yes,' she asserted. 'There was a problem, but it wasn't his fault and we managed to clear it up.'

'Uh-huh. That's nice.'

Liz found herself fidgeting, first with a letter opener, then with the retractable top of her pen. 'Well, it's always nice to keep a good contract——'

'—Especially if it means dealing with types like Mr Henderson. He is, as the kids would say, a real hunk. I wouldn't toss him out for eating crackers in bed!'

'I didn't particularly notice.' Her reply was prim, but her fingers performed a spastic tango quite unrelated to the staccato rhythm of her heart, and the pen flew in an arc, almost upsetting the dainty bud vase that held Con's carnations.

'Oops!' Janice reached out a steadying hand. 'Where'd you get such a gorgeous colour?' She leaned forward and inhaled the perfume of the flowers.

'I . . . oh, they were a gift.'

'From the sexy Scandinavian?'

Liz smiled, her tension almost dissipating in the face of Janice's unabashed and disrespectful curiosity. 'As a matter of fact, no.'

'Oho! I smell trouble in paradise. Is there someone new?'

'No,' Liz replied flatly. The badinage had suddenly become too personal and she drew down the veil of reserve that Janice had come to recognise only too well over the years.

'Okay. No more questions, except one: you're sure about this afternoon?'

'Positive.'

The Henderson penthouse was marvellously situated to offer panoramic views of the mainland mountains and inner harbour, clear across the Gulf of Georgia to Vancouver Island. Designed on two levels, with the bedroom an open loft looking down on the main living quarters, it was a sumptuous example of what unlimited funds and elegant good taste could achieve.

After she'd sent Nadine off to her dental appointment, Liz found herself touring the rooms, running her fingers over the plush velvet couches, the smooth, cool marble of the fireplace, as though she expected to pick up some invisible essence of Con.

It was all rather silly, she knew. This place was a business investment, a tax shelter. Con had probably never even spent a night here. But that didn't prevent her, after she'd arranged bouquets of huge white

chrysanthemums, from climbing the open stairs that
curved up to the loft, and indulging in some wild
fantasies at the sight of the low, wide bed covered in
burgundy satin.

Sinking down, she let her thoughts run free for the
first time she'd shown Con her door, giving full rein to
the longings she'd gone to such pains to stifle.

The dimness of the room, illuminated only by the
fading light from below, bestowed a close intimacy, the
silky fabric beneath her fingers poignantly reminiscent
of Con's bare shoulders. It wasn't true that men's skin
was coarse and rough to the touch—not all of it.
Unmindful of the creases she might be creating, she laid
her cheek down and rubbed it gently over the cover,
images of Con as he'd hovered over her the previous
Saturday flowing through her mind.

If Jens hadn't shown up when he did, she knew what
would have happened. She would have let Con make
love to her; she had wanted him to. And she still did.
There was a dull, heavy ache in her that nothing would
ease.

The rattle and clink of glass jerked her out of her
daydreams, and she bobbed up like a cork afloat to
restore the bedcover to its original geometric neatness
and run a smoothing hand over her hair. She was no
longer alone in the suite!

Daylight had slipped into dusk, and the room below
was suddenly flooded with the golden warmth of
lamplight, casting elongated shadows on the sloping
ceiling above her. Cautiously, Liz peered over the
railing, half-hopeful that Con was below, half-dreading
he might be.

Shoulders too narrow to be Con's topped by a head
of soft brown hair brought relieved relaxation to her
taut body. Pursed lips whistled an off-key rendition of a
current hit, then, as the last bottle was stacked in the
liquor cabinet, the visitor serenaded the suite with song
in a tenor more enthusiastic than tuneful.

Deeming it a good time to make her presence known,

Liz had one foot posed on the top stairs, all set to declare herself at the first break in the solo, when another arrival halted the performer in mid-warble.

'They're vacating the building in droves, pal—sounds as if someone's being murdered up here!' The rich baritone betrayed the identity of the unseen newcomer, and Liz froze.

'Hey, boss! I wasn't expecting you to show. Not checking up on me, are you?'

'Not exactly.'

Risking another furtive peep over the railing, Liz was favoured with a bird's-eye view of a second figure, the breadth of shoulder and night-black hair confirming what she already knew. Con had arrived.

He strolled over to the Pullman kitchen, his tall figure silhouetted in the track lighting from within. Casting a quick eye over its spotless counters, he prepared to turn away, then redirected his attention to the interior, disappearing briefly from view. Apparently satisfied, he came back to the living room, loosening his tie and running a finger inside the collar of his pale grey shirt as he did so. 'I am checking up, though.'

'Oh? Problems?'

'I hope not. I don't think so—not anymore. Pearson hasn't been around here, has he?'

Pearson! That, Liz now knew, was the name of the man Nadine had complained about.

'Not that I know of.'

'Good. I don't ever want him assigned here again.'

Con removed his charcoal grey jacket and slung it over the back of one of the couches. 'Everything seems to be under control, Dave, so why don't you take off? I'll lock up here when I leave.'

'Thanks. Sure there's nothing else?'

'Not a thing. I'm going to stretch out here a spell and unwind with some of that excellent Scotch you've stocked up on before I drive out to the airport.'

Liz's little gasp of horror echoed past her unguarded lips into the ensuing silence. Two pairs of eyes, one a soulful, enquiring brown, the other blindingly, heart-stoppingly blue, were raised to where she stood, half-concealed by the shadows in the loft. For a moment, all three remained frozen in a tableau of surprise, then Con stepped forward.

'Come out, come out, whoever you are,' he invited mockingly, and mortification stained Liz's face a dull red. Of all the embarrassingly stupid situations in which to find herself!'

'Just a second,' she replied, rallying her defences, refusing to slink down like a cornered thief. 'I'm not quite done up here.'

She gave the bedspread a final unnecessary twitch, aligned the lamp and ashtray more precisely, and bent back the cover of the book matches. Making no effort to muffle her footsteps, she marched briskly to the wardrobe, slid back the doors and swept the wooden hangers from one end of the rack to the other.

'Dave's gone, Liz.' Con's voice floated up, his obvious enjoyment of the whole escapade arresting her as she prepared to cross to the stairs. Oh Lord, she was alone with him—not what she'd intended at all.

'I'm not through checking over everything up here.' She had to play the part to the bitter end, and convince him her reasons for being up there were legitimate.

'Either you come down now, or I come up.'

'I'll come down,' she assured him hastily, eyeing the bed apprehensively. This was no place to have to face him! Trepidation gnawing at her, she set foot on the top step.

Even though, after last Saturday, he had decided to hold off and hope a little time and distance would work in his favour, he had not been able to pass up the opportunity to see her. When his secretary 'phoned the WREN Agency to make sure all the special arrange-ments for the foreign clients had been attended to, she learned that Ms Newman herself was stopping by the

penthouse to supervise the finishing touches—a morsel
of information she had tossed in Con's lap as carelessly
as a queen bestowing favours on a pauper. He had
wasted not a moment in turning the discovery to his
own advantage; an 'accidental' business meeting, he
reasoned spuriously, hardly amounted to the same thing
as a romantic encounter.

He'd known Liz was still there the minute he'd
looked into the kitchen. If the teal blue coat draped
over the breakfast bar had not been evidence enough,
the leather bag lying atop it discreetly initialled with a
gold LN had been added proof. It had taken him only a
second to identify her perfume clinging to the silver fox
collar of the coat. The assault to his senses had
electrified him. Desire had flared through his body in a
hot red flash.

He waited now, blanketing his response under a
façade of impassive amusement.

One slender ankle, ringed about with a narrow navy
strap, emerged from the shadows as a neatly shod foot
stepped with delicate precision on the topmost stair.
Slowly, a second foot followed and came to rest on the
step below, the gradual exposure of slender calf sorely
threatening his composure.

The full-skirted dress eddied away from her in the
gentle down-draught of her descent, teasing him with a
brief flash of scalloped lace stroking her thigh. From
this angle, the gorgeous limbs outran their normal
length, luring his gaze to undreamed of delights to
follow. At the turn in the stairs, she was facing away
from him and he seized the moment to feast avid eyes
on the vulnerable skin behind her knees and knew,
some day soon, he would explore that silken area with
his tongue.

Too soon, the staircase curved again and ended a few
feet from where he waited. An agony of desire inflamed
him, its throbbing reality leaving him hard-pressed to
maintain his calm demeanour. With an effort at control
she could never suspect, he raised his eyes from their

solemn contemplation of her knees and brought them to rest in mild enquiry on her face.

The heavy sweep of lashes veiled his gaze, still it scorched through the layers of her clothing, to brand her with its touch in the most secret and intimate places. She knew he had examined every emerging inch of her with the concentrated thoroughness of a connoisseur, missing nothing, taking note of everything.

Never hold up your underwear with safety pins! her mother used to admonish. What if you were in an accident?

She thanked a benevolent providence for her faultless turn-out now. If there had been a snag in her hose, a loose thread in her slip, Con would have known it. Decorously clad in a Bill Blass original, she had never felt more exposed.

The staircase had seemed interminable. She resisted the urge to rush down, fought the need to clutch the polished oak banister. Her pulse was racing, her knees trembling, but she would cut out her heart before she betrayed her humiliation and annoyance at being caught lurking in the loft.

She drew a deep, steadying breath, preparatory to tossing him an off-hand explanation of her presence, but he chose that moment to lift his gaze from its amused reconnaissance of her feet. The full impact of his brilliant blue regard travelled the length of her, sweeping the contours of her hips and blazing an undeviating path to her out-thrust breasts where it paused consideringly before coming to rest on her face.

A sweet, heavy languor invaded her, clogging the breath in her throat and bringing an aching awareness to her nipples, a sudden fierce contraction to the pit of her stomach. Desperate to disguise her raging response to him, she raised her drooping eyelids and met his gaze with unblinking resolution.

'I believe . . . everything is in order,' she murmured,

unable to dispel the huskiness that overlay her voice.
'Everything you . . . wanted . . . is taken care of.'

'Thank you.' He held her gaze a small, unflinching
eternity, releasing it only when the silence between them
grew almost palpable. 'I'm glad you're here. I was going
to call you later tonight.'

'Really?' Her tone conveyed nothing of her surging
pleasure at his words, nor the disappointment she had
harboured at his five day neglect of her.
Disappointment? No. Regrettably, petulance was more
accurate. She'd come to lament her impassioned bid to
be left alone once he'd shown himself altogether too
agreeable about honouring it. Didn't he know she'd had
time to recover from their last meeting?

His next words indicated that perhaps he did.
'There's a reception on Saturday—six to eight at The
Four Seasons—for our Japanese client and his wife.
Will you come?'

'I'll have to check my calendar.' It wouldn't do to fall
over herself with eagerness.

'Of course.' His response disabused her of any idea
she might have entertained that he was seeking her out
for the pleasure of her company. 'But I hope you'll
decide to come. You'll round out the group of lady
professionals I'd like to introduce to Mrs Hashimoto.
She's a product of an entirely different culture and I
think she'd be quite fascinated by you in particular.'

'Oh?'

'Yes. You're thé Western counterpart to the
traditional Japanese woman, except that you've turned
your skills into a paying business proposition, a
somewhat unusual concept for them, I suspect.'

So, she was invited along because she was a peculiar
specimen of womanhood! 'I'm not sure I can make it.'

His eyes remained unremittingly focused on her,
observing the slightest shift in facial expression, his ear,
she quickly realised, equally attuned to her tone.

'Are you afraid of me?' he asked.

'Certainly not! I'm just not sure about Saturday.'

'I see.' Derision glinted faintly in his eyes. 'What you probably mean is it's a lot safer to stay away from temptation.'

'And you see yourself as dangerously irresistible, I suppose?' she retorted witheringly.

'It's how you see things that matters, Liz. I think you're running away from the idea of us.'

'Your imagination's running wild.'

'Then show up on Saturday.' Under the insouciance, he was luring her to accept the challenge, and she rose to the bait, determined to prove him wrong. 'I will, provided I haven't forgotten some other engagement.'

'May I call you later to confirm?'

His studious politeness exasperated her. Where had all this mannerly circumspection been last week when he'd trailed out of her bedroom to flaunt himself, half-undressed, before Jens' disapproving glare? 'Please do. I'll be home any time after seven.'

'Thank you.'

Once again, silence threatened to smother them.

'I'll get my things and leave, then.' She turned away warily, expecting he would come after her, offer to help her with her coat.

He did neither, merely remained where he stood, his tall frame blocking her exit, making it impossible for her to leave without squeezing between him and one of the couches, his eyes following her every move.

He was daring her to brush against him as she left, defying her affronted glare which suggested that, had he been anything of a gentleman, he'd have stepped aside to make her exist easier. Then, from nowhere, he was assailed with a feeling of—what? Guilty paramnesia, for God's sake!—the illusion that he was resurrecting old pain for her, as evinced in the almost desperate gaze she flung at him as she attempted to scuttle past. Why did her actions strike such a familiar note? He'd never sent her packing, though at times he'd have liked to shake her for her resistance to his carefully engineered plans to seduce her. Inexplicably ashamed, he moved to give her freer access to the door.

She was almost past, almost returned to the safety of the outside world when he lifted his hand. She nearly flinched at the impending contact, unsure of so many things—his intentions, her expectations.

'It's cold out,' he commented softly, his eyes lingering on her lips. With courteously impersonal fingers, he turned up the silver fox collar, framing her face in its luxury. 'Good night, Liz.'

Tension clutched her stomach and swelled to clog passage to her throat as she rode the elevator to street level, all memory of her avowed wish to end their relationship negated in the overwhelming impact of seeing him again. To have been so close that only their clothing separated them, to have brushed against the pillars of his thighs, felt his breath ruffle the fur around her neck, brought fresh yearnings to lodge in her heart. How empty all her fine accomplishments seemed beside them.

And overriding all else was his unpalatable acceptance of the terms she'd laid down with such righteous passion the weekend before. If they were to enjoy anything more than a bland business relationship, it was obvious she would have to be the one to bring about the change.

I believed I had enough—a successful business, social acceptance, physical glamour—to be able to forfeit the other things, she thought miserably, as she prepared a lonely dinner for herself later that evening. I truly believed I could settle for less than anyone else, that I didn't need to be close to someone to be happy.

Someone? She pushed her plate away, regarding the grilled chicken leg with marked disfavour. Someone? She didn't need someone, she needed Con. So what was it that made her shy away from more intimate involvement, she asked herself, and knew at once that it was fear: fear of taking a chance, because she'd be gambling with her whole life; fear of having to deal with the unavoidable complications of her and Con's mutual past.

She'd have to explain that she was Willie Newman, the gauche girl from Cannon River, the girl on the beach; the girl who'd shown such a marked lack of self-restraint that she let a near-stranger lay claim to her body without having the wit to protect that body against the consequences of her folly; the girl who, having compromised herself beyond all hope of parental understanding, felt even more of an outcast by Con's apparent indifference to her. For, by the next day, she knew what had driven him to seek consolation from her: the Hendersons were a family turned in on themselves in grief for the senseless waste of a beloved older son and brother, in some alien jungle half a world away.

Memory stained her cheeks with hot red mortification. How could she bear the shame of such an admission, how diminish the pain of remembering the cost to her in the months that followed?

Resting her hands flat on the surface of the counter, she pushed herself upright, noticing with frustrated impatience that she'd unconsciously picked at her nails to the point that her manicure was ruined, the polish chipped and ugly. Oh, this was regression of the worst kind! Among her other little vanities was the habit of keeping her hands faultlessly groomed. It was another of her sacred status symbols never to permit the slightest resemblance between her dainty fingers and the rough, red little paws that had been the legacy of Willie Newman, housemaid.

Her life, she observed with bitter irony, was a mass of superficialities and pretence, threaded on the string of the one honest emotion she was finally forced to accept: that of her constancy to Con, whatever the past.

The 'phone rang and she reached out an eager hand, then regretted not showing more restraint when the caller identified himself as Con.

'Hi!' came his casual salutation. 'Everything's set for Saturday night, except for you. How's your calendar? Will you be there?'

The bubonic plague wouldn't keep her away! Suddenly, the perfect solution presented itself: see him as often as she liked, but always in the company of others. Thwart his every effort to get her alone. That's when she became unmanageable, a slave to her heart, her wayward, disobedient body. She would permit him, for now, to be her princely consort! 'Yes. I'm looking forward to it.'

She waited expectantly, eager to assert her independence by declining to have him collect her. She'd arrive under her own steam, and forestall any plans he might be hatching for a cozy exchange in his car.

She couldn't fend him off indefinitely, of course, but if she could buy a little time, just enough to see how well she coped, it would help. She needed time, time to come to terms with this disturbingly *decent* man. He'd changed in twelve years; she had, too. Maybe now, things *could* work out for them. Then again, she might, on closer acquaintance, find him entirely resistible. Oh joyful thought!

'Wonderful,' he replied briskly. 'I'm sorry I won't be able to stop by for you—I'll be tied up with the visitors—but I'll send a car for you.'

Deflated, she thanked him rather bleakly and assured him she could manage her own transportation.

'Nonsense. I won't hear of it.' He dismissed her offer out of hand. 'A driver will pick you up at a quarter to six.'

Riled by his dictatorial manner, she none the less let it pass, her mind already skimming ahead to the coming weekend and what she'd wear. It was amazing how reaching a decision on how to deal with Con injected her with such optimistic energy, instilled new confidence in her ability to handle a limited relationship with him.

It had been thoroughly exhausting, this game of advance and retreat she'd been playing with him, like some silly bird uncertain of its proper mating rituals. She was done with swinging from utter denial of him to covert craving for him. Clever Liz had devised a way to achieve the impossibe—to have her cake and eat it, too.

Con the consort! The title had a light-hearted nonsense to it that helped banish her unease at the tone of their 'phone call. She'd expected him to be far more gratified at her acceptance of his invitation. His equanimity at receving the joyful tidings had been a trifle disconcerting!

Poring over the contents of her wardrobe later, she searched for something appropriate to wear on Saturday, sifting through the rack of outfits with a dissatisfied frown wrinkling her brow. She wanted something distinctive, gracious ... memorable, and could find nothing that quite fit the description.

In the end, she went shopping on Friday evening, and came home enormously pleased with the purchase of a Halston cocktail gown in soft violet silk. The epitome of good taste, it was yet a subtle show stopper, artfully draped to reveal a minimum of skin, but clinging with such stunning fidelity to all the right places, proclaiming *woman* with such unabashed pride that even the most jaded eye could not fail to take a second look.

She may have determined that, where Con was concerned, there was safety in numbers, but it didn't prevent her from wanting to impress him. If he was entertaining notions of presenting her as a professional domestic with all its attendant connotations, he was about to discover that she was equally at ease in his elevated social circle. Dressing the part was only half of it.

At some point in the last few days, battle lines had been drawn up between them. She was going to lay siege to Con's cool composure and found herself suddenly eager for the parry and thrust of covert flirtation with him. After so many barren years, the zest of the game intoxicated her. This time, though, she would exert some control instead of settling for the role of lamb on the sacrificial altar. Willie had been pitifully passive. Liz was of an altogether different breed, and this time around, Con wouldn't have everything his way.

CHAPTER SIX

THE dress wrapped her about in cobweb fine luxury, its sheen almost outrivalled by the polished glow of her hair, its deep amethyst lending hints of muted lilac to her blue-grey eyes. Not in the habit of using clothes as a screen to mask her insecurities, Liz was surprised at the comfort she took from knowing she looked her best.

It had proved quite an ordeal to brave the formal receiving line alone, aware that, as she exchanged greetings with the Hashimitos, Con was taking flagrant inventory of her from head to toe.

Immediately the introduction was completed, he had turned her over to a Sam Fiedler, explaining in an aside that it was unlikely he'd be able to afford her much personal attention because of his responsibilities as host.

'I'll find time to bring Madam Hashimito over to you later,' he offered, almost by way of consolation, and she managed to bare her teeth in a facsimile of a smile before being borne away by the dutiful Sam.

She had not come prepared to be foisted off on one of the Henderson minions! If Con was otherwise occupied—and it was reasonable enough that he should be, she admitted grudgingly—then she was perfectly capable of looking after herself.

She was mingling in illustrious company, after all. She had recognised a Supreme Court judge, a bank president, and the Japanese Consul and his wife in the group scattered around the small but elegant banquet room. Still at the door, Con was introducing newcomers to the guests of honour, a couple of inestimable dignity and composure who were presently withstanding the combined onslaught of an effusive

television host and his wife. To one side, the fashion
editor of the local newspaper was running an observant
eye over Madam Hashimito's exquisite kimono, and
making discreet notes on her cocktail napkin in
preparation for tomorrow's column. Eventually, she'd
turn a less kindly critical glance on the other ladies
present, and Liz was glad once again that she'd gone to
such pains with her own appearance.

A waiter presented himself for their orders, and at
Sam's enquiring glance, she chose her customary glass
of wine. As if he sensed her irritation at his hovering
presence, Sam cleared his throat and gazed around a
trifle wildly, obviously searching for a suitably
engrossing topic of conversation.

'Er . . . I gather you're a friend of Con's,' he began
hesitantly.

'More a business acquaintance really,' she responded,
and sternly dismissed from her mind the image of Con's
torrid kisses, bending her energies instead to making
Sam's thankless task less painful.

It was relatively easy. He was plainly flattered at being
singled out as her escort. It was equally obvious that, in
his estimation, Con enjoyed a status only slightly less
awesome than God's. She knew just how he felt. As a
girl, nothing had been able to inhibit her adulation of
Con, then a high school senior during her freshman
year, and later something of a legend on the college
basketball circuit. That he was also the second son of
mill owner Joshua Henderson had merely enhanced his
god-like stature to the adolescent Willie, who was
content to worship from afar, accepting without
question the unlikelihood of his ever noticing such a
lowly specimen as herself.

What element of his personality was it, she wondered
now, that elicited such blind devotion from his
admirers?

'How long have you worked for Henderson
Industries, Sam?' she enquired, the germ of an idea
forming in her mind.

'Almost ten years, but I only came to Vancouver the year Con took over as president up here.'

'Really?' She impaled him with a look of fascinated interest. 'Then you've know Con for quite some time. Has he changed much over the years?'

'In some ways, I guess. Haven't we all! But, you know, the thing about Con is he never lets things interfere with his work. No matter what sort of problems he might be dealing with outside the office, he's always there, on the job and available when he's needed.

'Maybe he's one of the lucky ones who doesn't run into too many problems.' She was blatantly fishing, but hoped he was too hypnotised by her rapt gaze to notice.

'I wouldn't go that far. He's had his rough spots, just like everyone else.'

It was apparent that Sam could wax eloquent on Con's virtues and universal popularity all night, but that was scarcely Liz's objective. To her shame, she was far more intent on learning about Con's personal life, but loyal Sam was not so bedazzled that he was induced to be indiscreet, and Liz was rather ashamed of her efforts to weasel gossip from this nice man.

'Well, here he comes now!' Sam's awed tone told her quite plainly that a visitation from the great man himself was imminent. Naughtily, she laid a hand on Sam's arm and leaned slightly forward as though to impart some private tidbit of conversation. It was preferable to the knee-jerk responses Con's presence tended to provoke.

'Sam, may I borrow Liz for a few minutes?'

It was not quite an order, and Liz was singularly unflattered at the alacrity with which Sam relinquished her. Obviously, when it came to compelling magnetism, she ran a slow second to the boss! She turned to find Con at her back, the diminutive Madam Hashimito by his side, one tiny porcelain hand tucked beneath his elbow.

'Miss Newman operates the agency I was telling you

about, Madam.' Con bent attentively to the older woman who raised liquid eyes to Liz and smiled shyly.

'I am so pleased, Miss Newman,' she exclaimed in careful English. 'Please tell me how you make your men pay money for such service.' She giggled charmingly, covering her mouth with her fragile fingers. 'In Japan, we must perform such tasks out of duty and respect.'

'So do we, Madam Hashimito, sometimes,' Liz replied.

'I've yet to persuade Miss Newman I'm worthy of such favours,' Con interjected, and took amused note of Liz's stunned reaction to his next words. 'Perhaps you can convince her to look more kindly on me.'

He excused himself and drew Sam to one side, and Liz concentrated with difficulty on the woman before her, finding her attention straying all too easily to where the two men stood with their heads together.

He'd assigned Sam to Liz in an effort to keep the other unattached men at bay, and Con was frankly irritated at how well the two of them appeared to have hit it off. It was time, he figured, to outline to Sam the full extent of his responsibilities and to make it clear where duty ended and poaching began.

It was tough enough to have to play this frustrating waiting game, without being subjected to the sight of some other man fawning all over her—even one of Sam's sterling character. That dress she wore was so damned indecent in its clinging propriety that it generated some alarmingly primitive urges in Con, not all of them directed at Liz. He could, he realised with a sense of shock, quite easily become violent with any man who was disposed to show her too much attention. And his reaction to the sight of her leaning towards Sam, her hand resting confidingly on his arm, had caused something sour and ugly to rise in Con's throat.

If this is the price of restraint, he thought ruefully, I may find it too costly to pursue.

He wished now he'd allowed himself the luxury of

including her in the entire evening's programme. It had been much easier to abide by his decision to wait for her to make the next move when she wasn't across the room purring at someone else.

'I'm tied up with a private dinner for the Hashimitos after this,' he informed Sam tersely. 'I'd like you to escort Miss Newman back to her apartment in the company limo and then be available later to arrange transportation for the Consul and his wife and daughter.'

It was dirty pool, effectively curtailing Sam's freedom so that, even if he were entertaining romantic notions towards Liz, he couldn't put them into operation. And alone in her apartment was the only safe place for her, as long as she was wearing that provocative outfit.

Oh God, the gentle curve of breast and hip, the barely defined sweep of thigh, overlaid with shimmering colour as pure as a rare jewel, was enough to drive him mad. He *would* have her—and not just in the physical sense. Somehow, he'd find the key to that opaque withdrawal, penetrate the lacquered perfection of her shell.

Whoever had first laid claim that all was fair in love and war had a pretty thorough understanding of a man's psyche.

It was only eight-thirty, and she was home for the evening. What a total waste of a Saturday night, not to mention the outrageous extravagance of the dress!

Resentment simmered as she carefully hung the gown in a plastic garment bag and stored it at the back of her wardrobe. She'd been picked up and delivered back again like ... a sack of laundry, and if it had been Con's intention to humiliate her, he'd certainly succeeded. That ridiculous excuse that she was invited for business reasons had been a patent fabrication. She'd been permitted a scant five minutes with Madam

Hashimito, and practically joined at the hip to Sam Fiedler for the rest of the time.

It was as if Con had hired a keeper for her, afraid she might behave inexcusably and disgrace him before his important guests. Why on earth had he bothered to invite her?

And yet ... and yet, she could have sworn, when she left with Sam, that there was something warm and proprietorial in the look Con cast towards her, in the lingering handshake he extended to her as he mouthed polite nothings in farewell. And that remark of his to Madam Hashimito—*convince her to look more kindly on me*, or something—was tantamount to a proposition, if nothing more! What was really happening behind that charming, sophisticated exterior?

If she were to be honest with herself, she had never expected the evening to end so soon. She had been prepared to accede to an urgent request to join Con for dinner, once the hoop-la of the reception was over. She had a well-rehearsed speech on hand, graciously declining his offer to see her home afterwards. She was primed for the role of lady-friend to the powerful and successful Conroy Henderson, prepared to project aloof pleasure in his company in just the right quantity to guarantee his temporary devotion. And then, if she proved sufficiently hardy, she'd decide whether or not she could afford to extend her favours to something less timid and lukewarm.

Indecision, she decided, was something she tolerated poorly at best. The vigour had disappeared from Con's pursuit of her, his persistence had faded. The cooling of his passion that had once seemed so desirable she now found totally unpalatable.

Had he wearied of her so soon, bored perhaps by her apparent inability to handle a relationship that wasn't entirely safe and platonic? Or was he merely honouring her wishes—and waiting for a signal from her that she was ready to progress to the next stage of an involvement with him?

There was, it occurred to her, one way she might resolve all this. She would issue an invitation, ostensibly to an informal dinner party, here in her home. Surely, if it was encouragement he sought, he'd recognise this as a positive sign and accept? If he had, in fact, decided to cut his losses and run, his refusal would be all that was needed to make his intentions perfectly clear.

She sat down at once with pad and pencil, and drew up a tentative guest list for the following Friday. She'd issue handwritten notes, mail them tomorrow and be in receipt of the replies by Wednesday. By next Saturday, she intended having a clear indication of where her relationship with Con was headed, or indeed, if they even had a relationship worth developing.

This was the last weekend she'd waste mooning over Con Henderson. That sort of behaviour didn't fit Liz Newman's image at all.

By Thursday afternoon, however, she began to think the whole idea was destined for disaster. One couple couldn't make it, and the silence with which Con had received his invitation left her dangling in indecision, robbing her of the energy to seek out replacements. She wished there was some way she could extricate herself from her obligations to the remaining four guests who would land on her doorstep at seven-thirty tomorrow expecting an evening of scintillating conversation and fine dining.

Two of the four were Janice and Sam. Both casual business connections, they would, she'd hoped, give credence to the mood she was hoping to establish: not too intimate, not at all significant; merely a sociable gathering of people with shared interests. The last impression she wanted to create was one of couples entrenched in cosy togetherness. God forbid Con should interpret the occasion as an attempt on her part to snare him.

Now, it seemed likely she had saddled herself with a group of people who'd probably hate each other on sight, and all as a cover for her devious efforts to divine Con's feelings for her.

What an absurd mess she'd created with her machinations! Lassitude warred with annoyance as the sheer folly of the whole endeavour stared her in the face. Dispiritedly, she ran a line through her projected menu, the stuffed game hens she'd planned seeming entirely too pretentious to be served at such a calamitous event.

Kentucky Fried Chicken, anyone? she wondered caustically, and caught herself chewing a fingernail. What did Con's silence signify? There was no private address listed for him in the 'phone book, and she had been just as glad to mail his invitation to the office. It helped preserve the illusion of casual business-contact socialising. Sam had also received his invitation at work. Sam had 'phoned his acceptance on Tuesday.

Ignoring an invitation was inexcusable rudeness; it was unacceptable behaviour at best. Was it, in this case, a calculated insult? Was it a repeat of the blank dismissal she'd been issued after she'd served her purpose as a teenager in Cannon River?

The intercom broke her increasingly bleak chain of thought. Glancing at her watch, she depressed the flashing button and lifted the receiver. It was almost four-thirty; she'd have to leave soon if she was to take care of the shopping for tomorrow.

'Yes, Sheila?'

'Mr Henderson on line three, Liz.'

'*Con* Henderson?' Cautious anticipation prickled over her skin.

'The one and only. Will you take the call or shall I take a message?'

'I'll take the call.' She reached forward and made the line connection. 'Liz Newman,' she announced, carefully projecting her most neutral business tone. This was, after all, a call to her office in the course of a normal working day. No reason to hyperventilate.

'Liz! You're still there!' Con's voice, anxious and relieved at the same time, filled her with embryonic optimism.

'Hello, Con,' she responded briskly, absolutely nothing of her previous inertia or despair evident in her voice. 'Where else would I be?'

'Oh hell, I don't know, I'm just glad I caught you. Listen, I've been in Seattle since Monday and got back about half an hour ago. I've only just come across your note among my mail. Am I too late to accept for tomorrow?'

Never too late, sang her ebullient and forgiving heart. She should have guessed there'd be a reason for his silence.

'Of course not,' she assured him, as though last-minute replies to her elegant soirées ruffled her calm not at all. 'I'm glad you're able to make it.'

'Just as well!' She could almost see the grin that accompanied his words. 'I'd show up anyway. Leaving a lady stranded isn't my style.'

Did he perhaps think this was an evening planned for just the two of them?

'We'll look forward to seeing you,' she replied pointedly. 'About seven-thirty, okay?'

'Oh! Wonderful. And Liz——'

'Yes?'

'I'm sorry I took so long to get back to you. It couldn't be helped, honestly.'

The euphoria held through the preparation of stuffed veal tenderloin to the lighting of candles on the black oak refectory table in her dining room. The apartment glowed with warmth and soft colour, exactly the right degree of tantalising aroma filtering through from the kitchen, precisely the most soothing volume of music drifting from the stereo.

Then the doorbell rang and her composure fled. This was so much more than just a dinner party. It was the night that could mark new beginnings for her and

Con—or signal an end she couldn't bear to contemplate.

Con was the fourth guest to arrive. She opened the door and locked her knees in an effort to still the storm of pleasure that swept over her at the sight of him propped in the doorway.

'Hi,' he murmured, and, in a single word, encased her in such shared and secret intimacy that she immediately regretted her cowardice in inviting other guests.

'Hello.' It was all she could do to reply, for his eyes were stroking her face, lingering on her lips in a way that snagged the breath in her throat and turned her heart over. 'Come in.'

She stepped back to allow him entry, inhaling the elusive fragrance of his aftershave, and fighting the urge to run a hand along the lean line of his jaw. An instant prisoner of his magnetic force-field, she found her whole perspective of the evening shifting. With the myriad obligations of a hostess confronting her, she faced the unadorned knowledge that all she wanted was time alone with this one man; time to explore the limits she had imposed on their relationship; time to explore the possibilities that lay beyond the safety of repression.

Con handed her a bottle of wine and inclined his head towards the living room. 'Sounds like quite a party,' he commented.

'Yes. Come and let me introduce you.'

She turned away, breaking that debilitating eye contact, and prepared to lead him in to the others. The doorbell halted her progress and he waved her away.

'Answer it. I'll introduce myself.'

It was an evening of searing intensity interspersed with the total relaxation that only good food and good company can promote. It gave Liz the utmost pleasure to observe Con across the room from her, casually leaning against the mantelpiece, assuming responsibility for keeping the fire fed. That the other women were equally charmed by him was of no consequence, for she knew that he reserved for her alone that brilliant unblinking gaze and slow smile that warmed her every place they touched.

Later, from the safety of her position near the window, she allowed herself the luxury of a slow and careful survey of his elegant length, sprawled in cushioned comfort as he debated some point with Sam. His pearl-grey suit offset the black hair and vivid blue eyes, enhanced the amber skin, showed off the athletic lines of his frame.

His hand gestured eloquently, then he abruptly straightened, tugging at the knees of his trousers as he leaned forward to emphasise a point, and Liz's gaze was drawn inexorably to the sculpted line of thigh, the unmistakably masculine curve of him revealed by the taut fabric. When he suddenly raised his eyes and captured her gaze, she flushed guiltily, knowing he'd caught her in a most immodest scrutiny.

Having six instead of eight for dinner had created something of a seating problem. Faced with placing Con at the head of the table opposite herself, or seated either to her left or right, she had opted for one of the latter. She didn't want him to feel singled out as her special dinner partner.

She had reason to regret her decision as the meal progressed. Though Con joined blithely in the dinner conversation, under cover of the table his knee came into frequent and prolonged contact with hers. It was more than she dared do to raise her eyes, certain that everyone present would be immediately suspicious of the feverish light in them. Instead, she concentrated fixedly on maintaining a steady hand as she lifted her wineglass to lips parched with anticipation and desire. She had no lasting recollection of a single topic discussed during the meal.

After, she was sorting through her LPs for a recording of Piaf's last concert, requested by one of the guests, and knew the instant Con joined her. Leaning over the cabinet, she felt the warmth of his regard, the actual heat of his body at her back. He rested one hand on her shoulder,—oh so casually—and curved over her, his breath fanning her cheek as he spoke.

'Having trouble finding it?' he enquired. 'Could it be at this end?' So saying, he reached his free hand in front of her and in doing so, pressed himself ever so slightly to her. It was the briefest of contacts, but she was electrified by his thighs at her hips, the width of his shoulders that fleetingly obscured her from the others in the room.

'I . . . have it,' she replied, her words exhaled on a near sigh.

'Wonderful,' he breathed, and in lifting his head, ran his lips over her hair.

A flush of joy raced from the pit of her stomach to her breasts, a faint residue sliding up her neck and lingering on the high angle of her cheekbones.

'Allow me,' he murmured and took the LP from her trembling fingers to set it on the turntable.

Liz didn't know quite how she expected the party to end, but when the first guest made a move to leave, anticipation rose high in her heart. At last, the real business of the evening could commence. She and Con would shortly be alone and free to explore new dimensions in their relationship.

Everyone seemed to stand at once and she endeavoured not to rush people into their coats. So anxious was she to see the last of the other four, she paid scant attention to Con's activities. When she turned from bidding the last couple good night, the sight of him buttoning his jacket and clearly intending to follow them struck her with the force of a blow.

'It's been a marvellous evening,' he told her, one hand on the door knob.

Disappointment the size of a grapefruit welled up in her throat. 'You're leaving?'

She shouldn't have asked, should have had the wit to mask her dismay, but the words were out before she could prevent them.

For a long moment, he looked down at her. He was

so close, she could see the shadow cast by the curving black lashes, could almost count each silky hair. To her enormous shame and distress, the vision faltered and blurred. Oh God, surely she wouldn't let him see her cry! Where was her pride?

'Is there a reason for me to stay?' His voice came strangely to her ears, rough and husky.

I want you to! She wished she could say it, longed to break free of the inhibitions that held her rigid in the face of his imminent departure. '. . . No. I guess not.'

'Ah. Then I won't presume on your hospitality any longer. You've had a busy evening and you must be tired.' Still that strange, congested tone to his voice.

He had the door open, had taken a step towards it, then suddenly stopped and faced her. 'Good night, Liz.' He brushed a kiss over her lips and turned away.

He was over the threshold, his back blocking her view of the empty hall. His hand released its hold of the handle and in another second, the door would swing closed behind him.

Something fierce and strong and incredibly painful fought to surface in her, and not all her tensed muscles or willpower could resist its final thrusting burst of power as it erupted free of her.

'Please . . .' she heard herself whisper, the words half-choked on a sob, '. . . . please, don't go.'

Win "Instantly" right now in another way

...*try our Preview Service*

Get 4 FREE full-length Harlequin Presents® books

Plus this elegant jewelry bag

Plus a surprise free gift

Plus lots more!

Our love stories are popular everywhere...and WE'RE CELE-BRATING with free birthday prizes—free gifts—and a fabulous no-strings offer.

Simply try our Preview Service. With your trial, you get SNEAK PREVIEW RIGHTS to eight new HARLEQUIN PRESENTS novels a month—months before they are in stores—with 10%-OFF retail on any books you keep (just $1.75 each)—and Free Home Delivery besides.

THERE IS NO CATCH. You're not required to buy a single book, ever. You may even cancel Preview Service privileges anytime, if you want. The free gifts are yours anyway, as tokens of our appreciation.

It's a super sweet deal if ever there was one. Try us and see.

HARLEQUIN PRESENTS

FREE GIFTS—FREE PRIZES

YES I'll try the Harlequin Preview Service under the terms specified herein. Send me 4 free books and all the other FREE GIFTS. I understand that I also automatically qualify for ALL "Super Celebration" prizes and prize features advertised in 1986. I have written my birthday below. Tell me on my birthday what I win.

WIN A GREAT PRIZE

▶ If you are NOT signing up for Preview Service, DO NOT use seal. You can win anyway.

FILL IN BIRTHDAY INFORMATION BELOW

MONTH   DATE

this month's featured prizes—a fabulous Island in the Sun vacation for 2 + as an added bonus for 101 lucky entrants, exotic & delightful Perfume Collections, direct from France.

PLEASE PRINT

108 CIP 8508

NAME

ADDRESS   APT #

CITY

STATE   ZIP

PLEASE PICK VACATION SPOT YOU PREFER ☐ BERMUDA ☐ ST. THOMAS ☐ ACAPULCO. Gift offer limited to new subscribers, one per household, and terms and prices subject to change.

IMPORTANT REMINDER:
Use "Sun" seal ONLY if you are signing up for Preview Service & want a chance to win this and all 1986 "Super Celebration" Sweepstakes prizes & prize features. Otherwise, mail card without seal.

If card is missing write:
Harlequin
"Super Celebration"
Sweepstakes
901 Fuhrmann Blvd.
P.O. Box 1867
Buffalo, NY
14240-1867

Harlequin
"Super Celebration" Sweepstakes
901 Fuhrmann Blvd.
P.O. Box 1867
Buffalo, NY 14240-1867

PLACE
1ST CLASS
STAMP
HERE

CHAPTER SEVEN

THE pressure that moments earlier had trapped the oxygen in his lungs eased so that air escaped through his lips in a soundless whistle. He took a second to gather himself together, then pivoted on his heel and looked searchingly at her.

She stood as though transfixed in a nightmare, her hands clasped in some sort of unanswered prayer, her eyes shut tight to ward off whatever horrible thing confronted her. A multitude of emotions assaulted him: remorse, shame, overwhelming tenderness. Good God, he was playing mind games to feed his ego; his gamble had finally paid off—but at what cost to her?

Liz counted the silent seconds and wished she could die. Shivering chill spread to her arms, her legs, and, despite her efforts to contain it, rattled her bones until her whole body shook. What sort of madness had taken possession of her, that she would bare her soul like this to Con Henderson of all men?

Go! Go! She willed him to move away far enough to let the door close between them and spare her the shame of having him witness her abject misery.

Sensing he was about to shake free of the immobility her words had visited on him, she clenched her eyes shut, unwilling to face his distaste at her maudlin display. How gauche and embarrassing he must find her behaviour.

And then, incredibly, his arms were around her and she was held so firmly to his chest that, even through her distress, she could hear the accelerated thudding of his heart.

'That's all I needed to hear. That's all.' His voice bathed her in tenderness, his hands gentling her until

the seething turmoil within subsided. Tears devoid of
sobs or sound overflowed her eyes and ran in silent
rivers down her face, washing away all the pretences of
the last weeks. She was left entirely spent, as exhausted
as some frail bird at the end of an arduous migration.

At last he stirred. Containing her within the shelter of
one arm, he closed the door, led her back to the living
room and settled her on his lap in one of the fireside
chairs. The carriage clock on the mantel ticked away
the minutes and still he held her, his hand stroking her
hair, his lips at her forehead. A log shifted in the
fireplace, splintering red sparks up the chimney, and
from the street below came the occasional swish of tyres
on wet roads.

I could stay here forever, she thought. I could grow
old with this man and never regret the passing of youth.

'We have a lot to talk about,' he murmured.

What was it that prompted her acquiescence? Battle
fatigue, or the knowledge that whatever it was that
bound her to him—obsession, addiction, love—was too
great for her to withstand any longer? It didn't matter.
In asking him to stay, she'd made her decision to risk
telling the truth, knowing that if he accepted it, there
was no limit to what they might create from this
precarious enchantment.

'Yes, we have,' she replied. So much more than he
realised was needing to be said.

'But not tonight. You're worn out.' She stirred in
protest, and his hand stilled its soothing motion to hold
her head captive against his shoulder. 'Tomorrow,' he
promised. 'I'll call you around noon and we'll spend the
rest of the day together, just the two of us.'

They were the sweetest words in the English
language: just the two of us. She rolled them round her
somnolent mind, drowsing in the comfort of their
shared intimacy.

'Mmm . . . that'll be nice.'

'Sleep first,' he announced, and scooping her up, got
to his feet then, with agonising slowness, lowered her

until her toes touched the rug, trailing her down the length of him until she was most thoroughly acquainted with the details of his form.

'See me out,' he whispered on a note of urgency, 'now.'

But how could she act on words that were promptly elbowed into oblivion as his lips slanted down to meet hers in a kiss so devastatingly thorough and prolonged that it robbed her of all strength? She melted into the angles of his body, drained and sated at the same time. Desire had not lessened, but with the promise of tomorrow, she was appeased, content just to be held and cherished tonight.

'It's late,' he observed, his voice ghosting against her ear and leaving the warm condensation of his breath in its outer hollow. 'Maybe,' he continued, his agile fingers removing the pins that secured her elegant chignon so that her hair spilled free, 'maybe it's too late.'

His hands slid to her shoulders and, with insistent pressure, eased her down to the floor, a simple enough achievement with her bones reduced to insubstantial ecstasy under his ministrations. She sank with him in a graceful tangle of limbs, lips fused in another kiss—a different sort of kiss that spoke of hunger unleashed, of dominance and submission.

She was enveloped by him, moulding herself to him in answer to his urging, restless hands, inviting him to savour the texture of her mouth, eager to welcome the questing warmth of his tongue.

Desire raged to fever pitch. The blood rushed through his veins, a drumming counterpoint to the anguished labour of his breath. She was the most exquisite, the most elusive creature he'd ever known and suddenly, when he'd been ready to accept defeat, she'd turned to him with a fervour and need that matched his. He found himself grinding bone against delicate bone, gripping her with hands grown careless of their fragile cargo, and was shocked into restraint. He was responding to her with the savage force of a youth, caring nothing for the skilful art of lovemaking, the finesse of seduction.

Cool fingers of reason probed to where he had pushed it to darkness at the back of his mind, and drew forth the knowledge of Liz that had prevailed for weeks on his impatience. Intuitively, he knew she would surrender to him tonight, and that, if she did, she would retreat from him tomorrow.

He wanted so much more of her than just the solace of her body. It was the spirit of her—mysterious, proud, independent—the quality that, in combination with her fine intelligence, gave her such style, such depth, that gave him pause. To 'take' her now could cost him the joy of shared tomorrows.

Fleetingly, he remembered another time when he'd taken without a thought to return, then lived to repent the greed that had cost him the loving young creature who'd shown him such tenderness. It loomed up like a spectre to haunt him, the same willingness to give. It had been years since anyone had been so unstinting towards him—another time, another place, but so much sorrow to distort things then, whereas now, there was such cause for hope and joy. He would not repeat that old mistake with Liz. Once was enough for his conscience to bear.

Not for the first time, he faced the knowledge that this was no casual fling, no self-serving one-night stand. Lifting his head, he leaned over her and cupped her face in his hands. Her lips were like crushed poppies, he noted with some shame, bruised and swollen from his kisses. Slowing his breathing with a conscious effort, he examined the delicate fan of her lashes, gold-tipped against her cheek, the sleek arch of her brows, the small, straight nose.

'Elizabeth.' He uttered the name on a sigh and steeled himself to withstand her molten, lavender-grey gaze.

Perplexed, she surfaced from the whirling depths of

passion, her body still alight from his touch. Why had he stopped? What had she done—or not done?

She raised a palm to cup his jaw, the question plain in her eyes, but he caught her hand in his and pressed it to his lips.

'Not now,' he whispered between quick, reassuring kisses to her fingertips. 'Tomorrow. I won't 'phone.' Her eyes flew open in distress, and he hastened to clarify his words. 'I'll come by for you at noon.' Slowly rising, he pulled her to her feet. 'Wear something warm.' He encircled her waist and buried his lips in her hair, inhaling the fragrance of her, then resolutely held her at arm's length. 'I'm leaving ... now ...' He marched her to the door and flung it wide. 'While I'm still able to.'

He was there as promised, at noon on a Saturday of rare mildness and sun. It seemed ludicrous that Christmas was only three weeks away.

'Do I really need to dress warmly?' she asked him as she let him in the door. She was coiled tight as a spring, wild, exuberant joy battering at the fortress of her conditioned restraint.

'Absolutely.' He was devouring her with his eyes and she felt that betraying heat surge up from the soles of her feet to consume her. She, for so long the untouchable ice maiden, finally experienced a glimmer of understanding for what Janice so forthrightly described as 'having the hots' for someone!

'Yes, sir!' She sketched a salute and skittered away to the panelled doors of the hall cupboard, her heart drumming with excitement. 'Mink or mukluks?' She tossed a provocative glance over her shoulder and he responded to it with a gratifying zest.

In two strides, he was beside her. 'Mukluks,' he growled into her neck and pulled her against him so that her back was impressed on his front, inch for detailed inch. 'And long johns.' He nibbled gently on her earlobe. 'And gloves, and a toque.'

'Good heavens!' The quaver in her voice had nothing to do with surprise or alarm and everything to do with the powerful masculinity of him at her back. 'Where are you taking me?'

'You'll see.'

He handed her into the Seville, illegally parked at the kerb outside the front door, as if she were royalty.

'When are you going to tell me where we're going?' She sank into the soft suede upholstery and observed the passing scene as he headed for the park entrance.

'You'll find out soon enough, sweet pea.'

'The zoo? The aquarium? We're going to feed the polar bears and watch the whales have lunch?'

The smile that created such turmoil in her heart flitted across his face as he reached up to the visor above the windshield. Retiring behind a pair of sunglasses, he maintained an enigmatic silence.

'I've got it—I'm being kidnapped.'

'You're right.' He swung past the bowling green and the banks of the stream where Canada geese grazed on the still lush grass. 'Why don't you give your curiosity a rest and find us some music?' He indicated the console between them and she turned in her seat to sort through the cassettes stored there.

'I don't even know what kind of music you like.' She didn't know very much about him at all, only that he'd stolen her heart years ago and never given it back.

'Don't worry, I like everything in there. Surprise me.'

They had passed the entrance to the aquarium, she noted absently as she selected a George Benson tape. To their right, the north shore mountains rose clear against the mild blue sky.

'How long will it take us to get there?'

'Where?'

'There—where you're taking me.'

He was smirking like a little boy with a pocketful of grass snakes.

'I don't like surprises,' she warned him.

'You'll like this one.'

She turned to look out her window, and vowed she'd choke before she betrayed any more curiosity. Let him play his games if they afforded him so much pleasure! But she was smiling, too. Her nervous tension had evaporated in the sunlight and his light-hearted mood.

She was glad she'd worn her new sweater under the cream, fur-trimmed jacket. She knew the turquoise cashmere gave depths to her eyes, so that they seemed more blue than grey. Sexy had won out over sensible, and around Con, keeping cool was far more of a problem than staying warm!

Con swung the car into the stream of causeway traffic and headed for the north shore with all the aggressive confidence of the daily commuter, impervious to her nervous gasp, or the mildly agitated lady-driver behind him who slammed on her brakes as though she'd suddenly been confronted by a run-away lion.

'Saturday drivers!' He was amused by Liz's reaction. She was craning over her shoulder to see how real the possibility of a rear-end collision might be.

'That car's got Washington plates on it. You almost ruined someone's holiday,' she accused him, laughing just the same.

'Tourists, weekenders, women—they're all the same when it comes to driving.'

'I don't believe I'm hearing this!' She was pink with indignation.

Visible through the tinted lens of his glasses, the laughing blue eyes swept over her, and fastened on her mouth. 'Did I kiss you good morning?' he asked, reaching out a finger and running it lightly over her lower lip.

'For God's sake,' she implored him, 'not now! This bridge gives me the willies.'

'Does that mean later?'

'Use both hands,' she begged, eyeing the heavy two-way traffic on the narrow span connecting downtown

Vancouver to the north shore. Ahead of her, the snow-covered mountains loomed suddenly close.

'Oh gladly, sweet Liz—but in that case, it will have to be later.' He swung to the centre lane and took the exit west, vastly amused at the confusion his remark had generated.

'You're just trying to distract me, but I've figured it out.' She watched as they turned up towards the freeway. 'We're going up one of the mountains—Cypress Bowl, I bet.'

'You see any skis on the roof?' He cocked a quizzical eye at her.

'We're hiking around in the snow?' she asked doubtfully. Her suede boots would never be the same again.

'You don't sound exactly thrilled at the prospect.' They were on the highway and Con accelerated until the car was humming along a good ten miles over the speed limit. 'Relax and enjoy the view.'

She'd seen it before a hundred times, but it never failed to enthrall her. The highway hugged the side of the cliff, following the curve of the shoreline far below. Today, the cluster of islands across the blue stretch of the Gulf looked close enough to touch. It might have been the middle of summer, except that the heater kept the car comfortably warm, and outside, the alders growing alongside the road were starkly bare.

'We've passed the exit for Cypress Bowl,' she told him.

'I know. We're not going up the mountain.'

'Do you live out here?' The question tumbled out as the thought struck her that he might be planning to show her his home. She wasn't sure she could cope with that sort of exposure just yet. She had to keep reminding herself that this relationship was still in the experimental stage; that, charming and attentive though he may be, this was still the same Con who had brought such havoc to her life before. She planned to take this second involvement very, very carefully, one cautious step at a time. She must keep a clear head—and on his turf, that might not be so easy.

She wasn't, she reminded herself ruefully, exactly famous for the restraint she exercised when she was alone with Con. Last night . . . oh, last night didn't bear remembering, so close had she come to total surrender.

'Uh-huh. Down about there.' He nodded towards the shoreline just below them.

She pulled her thoughts back to the present. 'So you drive across that bridge every day? How do you stand it?'

'Easy. Commuters are well-trained and mannerly. It's the Sunday drivers and tourists and——'

'I know! I don't suppose you've noticed some commuters are women?'

'Ah, but they're not flaky little ladies terrified to take their foot off the brake. Some women are different.' His hand curled around the back of her neck, his fingers tracing lazy circles inside the collar of her jacket. '*You*'re different—unique.'

Briefly, he took his attention from the highway to glance caressingly at her. The now familiar conflagration in her blood flared up anew, painting her cheeks with fire.

You too! came her fervent but unspoken response. He was unlike any other man she'd ever known, a disconcerting blend of opposites welded into an absorbing whole: powerful, confident, arrogant; yet tender, sensitive, unassuming—and packaged so beautifully! How easy it was proving to fall hopelessly in love with him all over again. And how potentially disastrous! Could she survive the pain of separation again, should things not work out?

'We're almost there,' he remarked, signalling his intention to take the next exit.

In a matter of moments, they were following a winding road down to sea level, and eventually doubling back on themselves.

'Oh!' Comprehension dawned as he turned in at the entrance to one of the city's larger yacht clubs.

'You guessed!' The car sighed to a halt and he turned the full force of his most engaging grin on her. 'I hope you're a good sailor.'

'I hope so, too.' Intoxicated by his nearness, the beguiling smile, she fought to repress the surge of desire that swelled within her.

'Then let's go.' He was out of the car and around at her door, catching her hand in his and hustling her down the ramp and along the docks to where a youth of about sixteen was oiling the teak trim on a forty-six-foot sloop.

'All set to go, Tim?' Con leaped aboard and leaned down to offer Liz a hand.

'You bet. Everything just as you ordered, Mr Henderson.' The boy gave the trim a last going over, then stepped back to admire his handiwork. 'She's looking good, eh?'

'Great. You're doing a fine job. You interested in putting in a couple of hours tomorrow—general clean-up?'

'Oh sure. Thanks—I can use all the work you can give me.' Tim nodded to Liz and dropped nimbly to the dock. 'Have a good day, sir, ma'am.'

Con turned to Liz and held out his hand, palm upturned. 'Welcome aboard the *Fleetwind*. What do you think of her?'

Liz looked about her, dazzled by the gleam of brass and chrome in the bright sun. 'She's beautiful, Con.'

'Glad you approve.' He removed the sunglasses and lowered his lashes to ogle her slyly. 'She was my favourite lady—until recently.'

Her stomach tilted, then righted itself, but it was his meaningful glance not the rocking motion of the boat that was the cause.

With the skill she might have expected of him, Con cleared the yacht basin and hoisted the sails, reaching down, as they gained open water, to switch off the engine. Suddenly, there was no sound but the rush of water along the sleek sides of the boat, and the gentle sound of the wind in the sails.

'Warm enough?' he asked her, squinting into the sun and swinging the wheel to steer a north-westerly course.

'Oh yes,' she assured him and turned her face into the breeze, conscious of how isolated the two of them were.

'Then come back here and sit beside me.' He patted the space next to him, and when she hesitated, went on, 'First rule of the sea: unquestioning obedience to the skipper.'

'You should have mentioned that before we left the dock,' she retorted, but complied willingly enough with his request. After all, he was steering the boat and keeping an eye out for other things that might pose a hazard on the high seas. How dangerous could he be with all that responsibility? Still, she maintained a decorous twelve inches between them, hiding behind her own sunglasses and taking sneaky inventory of him.

How did he manage to look equally at home in an executive meeting or aboard this magnificent machine? Today he had shed the conservative three-piece suit for a navy turtleneck sweater and a pair of close-fitting denims that conformed to his limbs with graphic precision.

He lounged behind the wheel, steering their course with one nonchalant hand, as alert, behind his relaxed posture, as a watchful cat. And then, suddenly, he reached over, hauled on the sheet wrapped around the port winch and, like the well-behaved creature she was, the *Fleetwind* heeled into the waves and Liz found herself sliding across the intervening distance and coming up against the solid bulk of him.

'Mission accomplished,' he drawled, his free arm holding her fast to his side. Pleasure, pure and uncomplicated, ran rampant through her. All the negative aspects of their past, the possible hazards of the future, dimmed beside the glory of the present.

'We were going to talk,' she reminded him, confident suddenly of her ability to cope with a continuation of last night's developments.

'We will,' he promised. 'Over lunch, in about half an

hour. See that cliff over there?' He pointed to a spot on the island looming ahead. 'There's a tiny protected bay in there where we can drop anchor. At this time of year, we just may have it all to ourselves.'

He was right. The narrow bay was deserted, protected from weather and view by a spit of land on the seaward side. They might have been miles from civilisation, cocooned in the special, solitary silence of the ocean at rest.

'Hungry?' Con jumped lightly from the foredeck to the cockpit, having checked the security of their anchorage.

'Starving. It must be the sea air.'

'It is, and I've come prepared.' He held out a hand, and eyed her lasciviously. 'Come into my parlour!'

Laughing, she joined him in the cabin. 'Why do I get the feeling I'll regret this?'

The atmosphere, previously effervescent as sparkling wine, was suddenly charged with swirling undercurrents.

'Never say that,' he urged, his voice rough with tender passion. Holding her by both hands, he pulled her to him and closed wind-chilled lips on hers. 'Liz,' he murmured against her mouth, 'I think I'm in love with you.'

The unexpectedness of words she had long since despaired of hearing from him jolted her with stunning force. That her lasting kind of love—twelve years buried, denied—might not be unrequited was a concept too wildly wonderful to absorb all at once. A strangled, inarticulate gasp half formed in her throat.

'Ssh. Don't say anything, not yet.' His fingers were cool and firm along her cheek, but his lips had caught fire and were blazing on hers, his breath igniting an impassioned concerto in her heart.

His hands slid down her spine until she was enfolded in his arms. 'Beautiful,' he whispered huskily, lifting his head to examine her upturned face, '. . . perfectly lovely.'

'Con . . .' There were unmistakable stirrings between them that no amount of clothing could quite disguise. Isolation, proximity and hunger threatened to sweep them past a point of no return, and with something approaching desperation, she pushed away from him. 'We were going to talk.'

Releasing her, he ran agitated fingers through his hair, and closed his eyes on a shuddering sigh. 'You're right.' For a moment, he examined the tips of his navy sailing boots, the expression in his eyes hidden by the dark sweep of lashes. Then, he raised his head and smiled at her, and she released the breath she'd unknowingly suspended, her fear of his displeasure evaporating in the warmth of his regard. 'You're right,' he repeated, and slapped his hands together. 'Food first, though—right?'

'Let me help.'

The danger was past—at least for now. With easy camaraderie, they set out the provisions Con had brought along.

'This is a feast!' Liz was amazed at the contents of the small refrigerator. Smoked pheasant, pâté, a bottle of California chablis were lined up on the teak table. From a wicker basket, he produced a wedge of Brie and a cluster of pale green grapes.

'Impressed?' He grinned at her solemn assessment of the meal, her nod of agreement. 'Then this should knock your socks off!' Reaching down to the gimballed stove, he withdrew a loaf of crusty French bread, warm and aromatic from the oven, and presented it to her on a wooden chopping block with a ceremonial flourish. 'How about that!'

'Good Lord, you must have been slaving since dawn,' she teased, recognising the scrolled logo of a well-known bakery on a paper bag lying nearby on the counter.

'I have,' he lied unblushingly, and pushed the offending wrapper out of sight. 'I'm a man of many and varied talents, as you're about to discover. Watch this.'

He opened the wine with incomparable flair and brandished it aloft. 'Would you care to taste and pass judgment, ma'am?'

'No. Stop stalling and start pouring, or I'll eat without you.'

It was after lunch, as they sat across the table from each other, that the tenor of the conversation shifted from trivial to consequential.

The temperature was dropping as the afternoon advanced and Liz could not repress a slight shiver. At once, Con rose to his feet.

'Too cold? I could start a fire.'

'Here?'

'Sure. Haven't you noticed the stove mounted near the mast? Let's do that—we'll be more comfortable.'

He touched a match to the charcoal arranged in the brass-trimmed box, adjusting the damper until the flames were drawing strongly. Luxuriating in the warmth, she eased off her boots and wriggled her toes, stretching her legs out and leaning her head back against the cushions.

He settled himself beside her. 'Now . . .' there was a perceptible change in his tone, '. . . let's talk. It's time, don't you think?'

CHAPTER EIGHT

IT was what she'd been wanting for days, yet faced with the actuality of it, Liz found herself searching for ways to delay. He found her reticence alluring, was intrigued by her closely guarded privacy, she knew; would he be equally fascinated to learn of her beginnings—and the hand he'd had in shaping the later results?

Attempting to postpone the moment, she sprang to her feet. 'We should clear up the kitchen.'

'Galley,' he corrected her. 'And stop trying to avoid the subject.' He patted the space she'd vacated next to him on the cushioned couch. 'Come sit down and tell me where we're going.'

It wasn't the approach she'd expected. 'I'm not sure I know what you mean,' she hedged, perching beside him like some wary forest creature poised for flight.

He took her hand and laced his fingers with hers. 'I think you do.' He fixed her with his unwavering scrutiny, noting each fleeting expression as it chased across her face: the apprehension, the caution and finally, the impassive shuttered look. He knew them all well, had been fighting them for weeks.

Every time he'd tried to get closer, to find out more about her childhood, her family, she'd closed up, grown deliberately vague, put him off any way she could. Well, not any more. His voice brooked no further procrastinating. 'Why did you ask me to stay last night?'

Flustered, she turned away and gazed out the port window to where the cliff top rose and fell in rhythm with the motion of the boat. 'I don't know. I shouldn't have . . .'

'Liz!' His free hand reached out to imprison her chin, forcing her to face him, to meet his direct, uncompromising regard. 'Stop playing games; stop

111

fending me off.' When she didn't reply, he continued in a voice rife with frustration, 'Why is it so difficult for you to admit to needing me?'

'I hate to give in to weakness.'

'Weakness? The dark brows lifted in exasperation. 'Damn it, Liz, *I* need *you*. Does that make me less of a man in your eyes? What does need have to do with weakness?'

She pulled back, freeing herself from the painful grip of his fingers along her jaw. 'Maybe weak isn't the right word.' She shrugged dismissively. 'Vulnerable, then.'

For a moment, he watched her profile, noting the rigid tension of neck and jaw, the sombre angle of lips pressed firmly together. In the fading light, she was pale as a cameo, only her hair, caught in a soft grey scarf at her nape, giving off subdued sparks of colour.

He would not, he promised himself with renewed determination, let her retreat into that familiar hauteur that she wielded to such inhibiting effect. 'Is vulnerable so bad?'

'It can lead to terrible hurt.'

'It doesn't have to. Sometimes, you have to be brave enough to let go and trust.' He ran a gentle, seeking finger along her jaw, attempting to turn her to face him again.

He was dizzyingly close, his shadow blocking out the sun so that only his breath, fragrant with coffee, warmed her neck. His lips, lethal in their sorcery, drifted lovingly over her skin and came to rest at the corner of her mouth. 'Trust me, at least,' he coaxed, 'even if you can't trust anyone else.'

She gave an unexpected gasp and let out a laugh so empty of warmth or humour that he recoiled as sharply as if she'd slapped him. She swivelled around to face him. '*Trust you?*' she echoed with such cold irony that their eyes locked, then blundered apart again, embarrassed. She covered her mouth with fingers that shook. 'I'm sorry,' she mumbled. 'It's not as simple as you make it sound.'

The level brows rose again in brief bewilderment, then drew together in a frown. 'Have you never been in love, Liz?'

'I thought I was, once, a long time ago.' She struggled to sound detached, composed. Here was the perfect opening; with a few well-chosen words, she could uncover all her secrets. 'It was a singularly unpleasant experience I haven't been tempted to repeat.' Her courage deserted her, and the moment slipped away.

'I know the feeling. I've been misled very badly myself. Did you know I was once married?'

The question shook her out of her morbid introspection. 'Married? No, I didn't know that. What happened?'

'It was a disaster. I soon realised we shared nothing of importance. Eva was a clothes horse, a beautiful social butterfly who loved to party and who wanted me as her escort. I saw myself playing a far more important role. Ambition was my god. I wanted to be on the top of the corporate heap and was as much to blame as she when the marriage fell apart less than two years after it began. We were divorced six years ago.'

'And since then? Have you ever . . .?'

'Not by a long shot—until recently. There have been women, but there was never *someone*. Do you know what I'm saying?'

Oh yes, she was tempted to retort. I was one of your women.

'There was one other time, though.' The bright blue eyes hooded, peering inward to some dim memory. 'And I was *very* vulnerable. God, I don't think I've ever been so vulnerable before or since. But it was completely onesided; it meant nothing to her. And I *hurt*, but only for a little while.' He looked up and his grin blazed out in the dim light. 'Ego is a fragile thing when you're young. The blow to my pride left a dent that took weeks to heal.' He pulled her back so that she was leaning against him, her spine melding to the contours of his hips and chest. Wrapping his arms around her, he crossed them over her breasts and ran his hands up to her shoulders. 'But you make it all seem worthwhile.' He rested his chin on the crown of her head. 'I love you, Liz.'

Her heart lurched with the pleasure and the pain of his words. Was his declaration too little, too late? 'You hardly know me. How can you be so sure it's not just infatutation? How do I know I won't get hurt again?'

'We're back to trust again, love. I can't change what happened in the past; I can't erase all the bad things. I can't even offer guarantees for the future—there are no absolutes. But you can believe me when I tell you I'll never knowingly hurt you. I'm not a kid anymore, Liz. I'm a man who knows what he wants, and I want you.'

'You may want me, but there's more to love than that. I'm not interested in being chalked up as one of your women.'

'You're doing it again.' His voice swelled with frustration at her insistent cynicism, filling the cabin with his anger. 'Love isn't a single dimension between a man and a woman. It's not all lofty ideals, spiritual ecstasy between two minds. It's earthy and physical, too. There's nothing evil or perverted in my wanting to make love to you!'

She twisted out of his hold, her fear flaring into annoyance, and favoured him with a withering glare. 'Why don't you announce it to the whole world while you're about it.?'

'Good idea!' Eyes shooting sparks, he leaped to his feet and out into the cockpit. Straddling the sole of the boat with a foot planted firmly on each of the deck cushions, he grabbed the boom in one hand and swung back and forth from the waist. 'Hey, gang! I want to lure Liz Newman to bed and kiss her silly!'

'SILLY ... Silly ... silly. . . .' His words echoed in diminishing circles around the deserted bay. A lone seagull swooped across the sky, screeching approval.

'Did you hear me, world? I want——'

'You idiot, I'll throttle you!' She catapulted from the hatchway, scarlet with embarrassment, and flung herself at his knees in a disarmingly graceful imitation of a flying tackle.

'—to take off all her clothes and kiss every inch——'

'Stop! Con Henderson, I'll never forgive you for this!' Her attempts to grapple with him were as effective as a gnat attacking an elephant.

'—of her. I want——'

'Please!'

He surveyed her from his lofty perch. 'Please what?' he demanded in lordly tones, his eyes flickering with wicked merriment.

'Please lower your voice.'

'Are you sorry for doubting my intentions?'

'I'm sorry! I'm sorry!'

He eyed her balefully. 'You're not.'

'Oh yes, I am—truly. Please get down and behave. What if someone hears you?'

Lithe and laughing, he dropped down beside her and enveloped her in an unyielding hug. 'That's the difference between us, sweet cheeks. I don't give a damn who knows how I feel about you.'

She fanned the ashes of her mortally wounded anger, unwilling to capitulate so easily to his blackmail or his charm. 'What about how I feel?'

'You care about me,' he asserted with complacent certainty. 'Admit it.'

'Don't be so sure.'

He lowered his mouth to hers. 'Let me in, love,' he cajoled. 'Let me show you how much we both care.'

His lips destroyed her reserve, taking her chill defences and melting them in hot, hungry kisses that left her yearning towards him. 'Oh Con . . .' The words were born with difficulty, uttered on a note bordering on despair. 'I want so much to try—to dare.'

Exultation surged through him, scattering doubt and caution in its path. Swiftly, he lifted her into his arms, prepared to defy God and the elements rather than deny the rampaging passion unleashed by her hesitant admission. He would make her forget whatever— whoever—had brought that haunted shadow to her eyes.

Balancing his delicate burden carefully, he stepped down into the main cabin and through to the forward berth. The door swung closed behind him, cutting off light so that only the reflected rays of the dying sun filtered through the starboard porthole.

He laid her down on the wide bunk, and leaning over her, buried his lips in the luxuriant fall of her hair, released by his impatient fingers from its restraining scarf. 'Liz?'

He was going to make love to her *now*, unless she stopped him. One word, one gesture of denial at this point would halt him. But one moment longer, and there'd be no going back. Thank God! All the threats he'd posed were defused by his gentle, loving approach, by the heartfelt sincerity of his words. He said he loved her, and she believed him and knew she loved him, always had.

Seconds glided by as smoothly and seductively as his hands on her body, and she knew she wanted this moment, had wanted it with a deep, persistent ache, for weeks; to say 'yes' to love, with no reservations, no conditions.

Even if, later, it made for new hurt, new regrets, she knew right then that she did not want to die untouched by this ultimate ecstasy; not to wither into old age without the tender hand of loving passion having swept her soul and illuminated her body.

Her debts had been paid long ago. This moment, ripe with promise, fraught with possible danger, was worth the price. She had evolved from girl to woman, and a woman's love was braver than a girl's. A woman was more generous in her giving, more willing to take risks, more cognisant of the lonely consolation of abstinence when the heart swelled with the need to give. A woman accepted what a girl could not: it *was* better to have loved and lost than never to love at all. Liz at thirty knew what Willie at eighteen could never have understood: trust can thrive beside acknowledged risk. What a dreadful poverty of spirit to deny the promise of the one in order to avoid the danger of the other.

She lifted her arms to hold him close. Without a word she surrendered to him. It was time.

There were so many layers of clothing separating them and such desire escalating between them, the air shimmered. With trembling hands, he traced the contours of her face, then slid them down to uncover the gentle curves, the warm and secret hollows of her body.

Her lifted the sweater away with near reverence, laid eager lips at her exposed throat and let his hands ripple over her shoulders until, inevitably, they searched out her breasts. A sweet, slow agony rolled through him at her sudden gasp of pleasure. Gliding his tongue over the soft swell of her flesh, he reached for the clasp, and with fingers grown nimble from passion, unsnapped her bra. Her skin gleamed in the waning light, the roseate nipples blooming as his lips sought first one, then the other.

Dimly, he became aware that her hands had trespassed under his own sweater, that she was holding him to her, her palms flat and urgent on the smooth skin of his shoulders, then curving delicately to explore the muscled ridges down either side of his spine. Her touch, cool and precise, inflamed him.

With barely controlled hunger, he released the button at her waist, lowered the confining zipper that gave access to the satin skin of her stomach. Murmuring her name, he trailed his tongue over her delicate ribs, dipping into the scented warmth of her navel, then travelling again to where her pouting nipples waited to receive his homage. Her breath, shallow and rapid, fanned the hair on his brow, and his own laboured unevenly in reply.

Gently, terrified that this ultimate breach might startle

her into flight, he eased the tailored slacks over her hips, his thumbs, en route, catching her tights and briefs, banishing them, too. Almost timorously, his hands roamed the curve of naked hip, teased the tops of silken thighs, advanced and retreated from the most intimately guarded part of her.

Desire grew within her to a painful and glorious tension. She was full of eager, welcoming warmth, a quivering anticipation seizing her so that her fingers trembled as they explored the length and breadth of him.

He was so utterly beautiful, so dark and powerful and sure. Suddenly, a tiny panic threatened as she remembered that hers was the body of a thirty year old, no longer quite as untouched by time as it once had been. She wanted so badly not to disappoint him. She wanted *this* time to be wonderful for both of them.

He sensed her hesitancy before it was uttered and hastened to reassure her, stilling her protest with lips that ambled languidly to her mouth and hovered there to scatter random kisses. Her alarm, brittle and repressive, fled in the face of his tender patience. When he cupped his hands beneath her hips and gathered her to him, her arching response was as instinctive and hungry as his own hammering need. His tongue darted between her lips in playful skirmishes, flirting with hers until they joined in a fierce and frantic duet. When his hands slid in wonder a second time over the silken, secret flesh of her thighs, the last shreds of resistance scattered and she knew only a swelling heat that spread from the pit of her stomach to permeate the farthest reaches of her mind.

With a wild impatience, he flung off his clothes and poised himself above her, supporting his weight on an elbow each side of her head. His heart booming to an unbearable crescendo, he lowered his mouth again to hers, and with dreadful, hurting care, stormed the furled portals of her womanhood.

Time swirled, meaningless, as sensations new as the dawn and ancient as the tides swept her into their current. There was a moment of resistance; a spasm of near-pain lanced her. Then, the ripples began, fluttering at her farflung extremities, narrowing and intensifying until they hovered at the core of her, wild and powerful, on the very edge of detonation.

By some strange impulse quite unrelated to her whirling senses, her fingers clutched and sought, gouging desperately at the smooth, unblemished skin of his back. From his mouth, buried in the hollow of her throat, breathless, inarticulate words of love showered over her, then hung suspended until, with a groan of anguished ecstasy, his own imperative hunger gathered to flood through her.

The unearthly tension that held her in marvellous thrall lunged for an impossible goal and, miraculously, secured it. Seized in its wild vortex, she was flung over and over against the implacability of Con's assault, until, with an abandoned cry she scarcely recognised as her own, she shattered into flying fragments. The tempest released her, depositing her, spent and whimpering, in the languorous aftermath of its rage.

For long moments, there was nothing but the decreasing tempo of their heartbeats. At last, Con lifted his head and stared down at her, half mesmerised, half horrified. Feeling his close examination, she raised lids still heavy with love and caught the disturbed expression on his face. Her fingers, pulsing yet with the residue of ecstasy, navigated his cheek and traced the blunted line of his eyebrow.

'Liz . . .' He seemed at a loss for words and a flicker of apprehension flitted over her.

'Oh.' She closed her eyes against his unblinking stare. Had it been wonderful only for her? 'Didn't I . . .?'

'This is the first time for you.' His words dropped into the silence like an accusation.

Her eyes flew open, restored to clarity. 'No!' she insisted, unsure why virginity suddenly seemed such a scourge, but glad she could answer with such forthright honesty. What if he'd phrased his question differently? What if he'd said: Was I the first? 'But it's been ... a long time. I'm not very experienced.'

'Stop apologising.' His eyes were luminous in the twilight and very close, his voice rough honey in her ear. 'I'm not complaining, love—just rather ashamed of myself.'

'Oh, don't be,' she sighed. 'I don't regret a thing.'

'If I'd known, I'd have been ...' His words trailed off in such miserable confusion that she reached up and pulled his mouth down to her.

'Hush,' she murmured against him. 'It was wonderful.'

'Magnificent,' he agreed and ran his tongue over her lower lip. 'I think ...' he warmed to his task, his busy, clever hands performing minor miracles, '... the earth moved. Unless ...' his mouth was wandering down past her ear, exploring its outer shell, nibbling at the lobe, '... we were caught in the wash of a ferry.'

Her laughter was smothered in a gasp of pure delight as he turned his attention to her neglected breasts. Impossible, surely, that he could arouse her again so quickly when only minutes earlier she had been drained of every last particle of energy.

He moved against her, powerful and insistent. Nothing, it seemed, was impossible.

There was no wind, and daylight was long gone when the *Fleetwind* nosed out of the secluded bay and turned her elegant bow towards the illuminated north shore. Ahead, the night skyline of downtown flung the reflection of its thousand festive lights across the rippled water and up to the stars.

During the forty minutes it took for the diesel engine to propel them back to harbour, they spoke hardly at all. It wasn't just that Con was watchful for floating

logs, navigating with care around the barely submerged
rocks that fringed the shore. Snuggled against him,
warm in the shelter of his arm, Liz, too, was coming
home after years of aimless wandering.

Finally able, she realised, to come home to Willie, her
vulnerable, loving other half from whom she'd exiled
herself for so long. She was no longer Liz, dazzling on
the outside, empty on the inside. All Willie's sweetness
of spirit invaded her and merged with the rational,
mature Liz. For the first time in twelve years, she felt
whole—almost.

'What would you like to do tonight?'

They were in the car, taking the lower road back to
town. The digital clock on the dash showed it was only
just past six, yet it seemed much later. In the comforting
warmth, Liz was half dozing. 'Nothing strenuous,' she
murmured, and flushed at the wicked gleam of Con's
smile.

'You need feeding, love. You'll be surprised what a
good dinner will do to restore your energy.' He reached
over and ran a possessive hand up her thigh. 'I know a
place just down the road in the village. Nothing fancy,
but great food.'

The village, she learned, was a term left over from
years earlier when West Vancouver had been a summer
resort accessible only by sea. To their right, the library
displayed a tall illuminated Christmas tree in its glass-
fronted entrance. The main street was strung with
lights, and even the police station, she noted, sported a
holly wreath. It all seemed delightfully rural still,
despite the luxury condominiums along the waterfront.

Con pulled up before the square-paned bow windows
of a small restaurant. Under the protection of a
pavement awning, stone urns of geraniums defied the
calendar and bloomed scarlet with flower clusters.

The combined noise of voices and laughter almost
drowned out the recorded Christmas carols as Liz
preceded Con into the crowded interior. When they were

seated in a booth near the back and had ordered, he reached across the table and took her hand.

'You're very quiet. Is everything okay?'

'Yes, of course.'

'No regrets?'

'None.' But it was only half true. The full impact of her earlier realisation was nagging insistently at the fringes of her mind. She was *almost* whole again. It was the 'almost' that reminded her of what she'd planned to accomplish before the day was out. Some time during those sunlit hours, she had planned to tell him what had happened twelve years ago in Cannon River. A dozen times, she'd selected a favourable opening, only to let the moment skip by. It had been such an idyllic day, she'd hated to spoil it by dragging up the past. He seemed disposed to continue their relationship this time. Why take a chance of having him change his mind by revealing the outcome of their first encounter? And somehow, the day had slid by, and the most important thing they had to talk about remained unsaid.

Was now the right time, she wondered, and ran through the various approaches she might take: Oh, by the way, I let you make love to me once before, but you've forgotten. I lost my virginity to you, but I don't think you knew who I was at the time. Oh yes, and I got pregnant, but don't worry, I miscarried—actually, I can't have children, because of the complications of that first time.

For all the recent joy of Con's loving, the emotional scarring of her sterility came between them still. How could she ever describe to him the agony of her loss without bitterness welling up to sour her words and lay implications of blame on his conscience?

Face it, she told herself. There is no casual or graceful way to drop plums like that on an unsuspecting head.

The dilemma drew her into herself and away from him. Immersed in her own thoughts, she missed entirely his quick frown, the close scrutiny of his regard.

He turned her palm up and examined its pattern of fine lines. 'I have wanted to make love to you almost from the day I met you. All the time you were reading me the riot act in your office, I wanted to touch you. The first time I kissed you, I felt like a kid again—so full of wonder and gratitude at being alive.'

The first time you kissed me, you weren't much more than a kid, she thought mournfully. And I can't find a way to let you know without making it sound like an accusation.

'Sometimes, though, you seem to be holding me off and I was terrified I'd lose you to someone else. The night you met Sam Fiedler, I finally realised the extent of my feelings. I knew, then, that I wanted you to belong to me.' He wrinkled his brow in mock anguish. 'You put me through mild hell, hanging all over Sam in that purple dress.'

She snatched her hand away indignantly. 'I do not hang all over men, Conroy Henderson. That's not my style. Nor do I wear *purple!* Petunias are purple. My dress was amethyst. And how did you ever find time to notice what I was doing or wearing? You barely acknowledged my presence. Why ever did you invite me to that party in the first place?'

'To feast my eyes,' he teased, delighting in her reciprocal jealousy. 'I debated coming over after the business part of the evening finished.'

'Who stopped you?'

'You did. If you'd still been wearing that indecent dress, I'd have done my damnedest to get you out of it—and got my face slapped for the attempt. Do you know,' he went on conversationally, 'that outfit didn't show much skin, but it drove me wild the way it showed off you quite remarkably lovely . . . assets.' He grinned disarmingly. 'I didn't want any other man indulging in the same erotic fantasies I was entertaining.'

Once back in the car, threading into the traffic beading the span of the bridge to the city centre, Con could no longer stifle the anxiety that had surfaced during dinner. Underlying their light-hearted exchanges, he'd detected a certain withdrawal in her, and a sense of urgency gnawed at him. What triggered that invisible barrier? Why when they'd been so close, did she suddenly put such distance between them?

During their lovemaking, her commitment to him had been total, he was sure. He was still reeling from the recognition that Liz was an untutored as a virgin, but there had been nothing coy or contrived in her response to him. Her artless exploration of his body, her complete absorption in the magic of their union, had captivated him.

He was dangerously susceptible. So finely attuned was he becoming to every nuance of her mood, he could almost feel her slipping back into that shell of reserve that closed him out so effectively. If the prospect of becoming her lover had tantalised him, the reality of it enthralled him and left him taut with the fear of losing her.

He made no effort to draw up outside her apartment, searching instead for a spot to park overnight. Flicking off the ignition, he half turned to face her. 'I want to be with you tonight, Liz—please.' He laid his fingers against her lips, stopping the response he was afraid would emerge as a refusal.

Didn't he know he had nothing to fear? That, in submitting to him, she'd come to terms with her reservations about loving him? Didn't he understand that, for her, intimacy forged bonds of total commitment? Amazed, she realised he did not, that Con was not nearly as reassured by their lovemaking as she'd supposed.

'Please,' he repeated, and was overcome with love and gratitude at the uncomplicated generosity of her reply.

'I'm glad,' she answered. 'I want that, too.'

CHAPTER NINE

IT was all Con could do not to sweep her up into his arms and over the threshold like some triumphant bridegroom. The second her front door shut them off from the world, he folded her to him. Inhaling the fragrance of her, he concentrated fiercely on the scent of sea air and wild violets and tried to ignore the persistent throb of desire that fought to rout civilised courtship in favour of pagan passion.

'Could we,' he formed the question with strained care, 'have coffee or something?'

'We could,' she murmured against his lips. 'We could have coffee and liqueurs, or brandy. Which would you prefer?'

'Brandy.' His restraint threatened to snap at the slow undulation of her hips against his. 'And perhaps a shower.' A very cold shower, he amended silently.

'Help yourself,' she invited, trapping him in her serious, lilac-misted gaze. Her innocence was quite unfeigned, he was certain, and he stamped out the licking tongues of desire that taunted him with such merciless intent. Putting her from him, he strode abruptly the length of the hall to the bathroom and closed the door between them with quiet desperation.

Don't be an animal, Henderson, he admonished his quickening body, and thrust it under the punishing sting of the icy shower.

The living room was deserted when he emerged some fifteen minutes later, his ardour dampened, at least temporarily. A bottle of Camus and two Waterford snifters were set on a low table and a fire burned in the hearth, but of Liz there was no sign. Then he heard the muted rush of the shower and realised she'd followed his example.

Congratulating himself on his commendable restraint, he banished the flickering hunger conjured up by the mental image of her soaping her long, lovely legs, her firm, high breasts. He could accomplish more by turning his mind to the nagging unease that had crept over him during dinner.

For years, he'd questioned his ability to love without reserve. Ever since the shambles of his marriage, it had been depressingly easy to avoid involvement; to take the consolation of casual affairs and give nothing in return.

Today had been a gem beyond price, a confirmation of what he'd recognised weeks ago: with Liz, he'd found the sort of love he'd almost despaired of experiencing. In her, he had everything he ever wanted. So why was there a cloud hovering over his head?

Because, he acknowledged bleakly, although he was very sure how he felt, he had no such certainty about Liz. 'I love you,' he'd told her, and the extent of her giving told him she loved him, too, but it had not escaped his notice that she had yet to say so.

His old conviction that there was a problem returned to torment him. *Some*thing was always there, rearing its head just when he was beginning to believe he'd conquered it. He'd hoped, after today, that she'd be free. Apparently she was not—and somehow, he had to persuade her to let him share the burden, whatever it was.

He was sifting through her record collection when she returned, the mingled aroma of coffee and her perfume alerting him to her presence before she spoke. Idly, he glanced over his shoulder, then spun around, straightening abruptly, all his fine intentions to practise restraint vanishing.

She was wearing a blue satin négligé, luxuriously trimmed in maribou. Unable to tear his eyes away, he watched with fascinated awe as the rich fabric swirled about her, hinting at the soft femininity hidden beneath.

'I believe,' he murmured huskily, his control sorely

threatened, 'this is what's known as "slipping into something more comfortable".'

'I believe you're right.' The glance she tossed at him from beneath demurely lowered lashes was a blatant invitation. With languid grace, she crossed to the table, set the coffee tray down, and lowered herself to the couch, the frothy feather trim rippling around her throat and wrists.

'You minx! You're trying to seduce me.'

'And doing it rather badly, it seems.'

He cleared his throat, ran a tongue over parched lips. 'Badly?' His voice cracked for a moment. 'What do I have to do to convince you otherwise—grovel?'

'Not at all. Just come and sit over here instead of gaping at me from a distance.'

'You'll be sorry you suggested this,' he promised, crossing the room with alacrity. 'My shower . . .' The cool blue satin hummed with vibrant warmth where it touched her skin. Captivated, he loosened the ribbons that laced the bodice, and let his eyes follow his fingertip at it traced a path between her breasts. '. . . was a complete waste of time.'

The gown whispered down her body and lay in a puddle of satin at her feet.

The aftermath of loving, Liz decided much later, was, in its own way, as delicious as the act itself. Nothing had prepared her for the sense of fulfilment that saturated her being, the closeness she shared with Con. The years of empty, yearning nights might never have been. Except . . .

Except for the moment, earlier, when Con had carried her through to the bedroom. Dazed with quivering pleasure at the explorations of his tongue over her body, she'd been tossed rudely to earth by his sudden discovery of her scarred abdomen.

'What happened?' He ran a gentle, inquisitive fingertip over the silvery line, just visible in the lamplight.

Panic left her temporarily bereft of speech. This was
not the moment for the truth. The facts surrounding her
ectopic pregnancy and the subsequent loss of her ovary
were only the prelude to the much grimmer fact of the
lingering uterine infection which had left her sterile.
She *would* tell him the whole story, and soon, but not
from this prespective. She wanted him to know the
truth; she wasn't interested in burdening him with
useless guilt.

'Appendicitis ...' She offered the lie with little hope
it would be accepted. A child would know the appendix
was located on the right side.

'Is that so?' Con had scattered kisses over the
incriminating evidence. 'My brother's was on the left
side, too.' How trustingly he'd accepted the explanation. And why not? Why should he suspect her
honesty?

Was that why she lay awake now, she wondered. A
simple explanation of their original meeting in Cannon
River, overlaid as it was with lies of omission, was fast
becoming an impossibility. To add a deliberate untruth
now seemed a sin of unforgivable magnitude. 'What a
tangled web we weave, When first we practise to deceive'
indeed!

This could cost you everything you've worked for,
her restless conscience warned. Sooner or later, you'll
have to pay, not just in heartache, but in loss of self-
respect; worse, in the loss of Con's respect. Why take
the chance? Why throw away everything for an affair
that can never last?

'Why' doesn't matter, her heart replied in swift
rebuttal. To live again is enough. If there's a price, you
can pay it later. It can never be as costly as the first
time. You don't have as much to offer—or to lose—
now. And it *might* work out. It didn't have to end in
disaster.

For the first time in twelve years, the needs of her
heart outran the demands of her head, and she turned
a deaf ear to the nagging of her common sense.

Shifting stealthily on her side, she let her eyes roam lovingly over Con. In the dim light from the street, she could discern the even rise and fall of his chest. It was the first time she'd seen him asleep, and it moved her to new heights of tenderness. Even at rest, he emanated power and energy, but the gentleness and sensitivity she loved were more apparent in the soft relaxation of his mouth. How strong he was, how beautiful, in his splendid, sculptured symmetry.

Fascinated, she explored with her fingertip the dusting of fine black hair that haloed the flat, masculine nipples, following with increasing absorption its narrowing path until it disappeared beneath the sheet pulled taut across his lean hips. Then, realising the rhythm of his breathing had altered, she raised her enchanted gaze, and inhaled a small gasp of shock. His eyes had opened and were gleaming darkly at her in the gloom.

She would have withdrawn her hand but he pressed it to him and held her palm against the stirring warmth of him. Coherent thought fled before the persuasive pressure of his other hand urging her down until she was crushed against him. Desire, sensual and untamed, harnessed itself to a wealth of tenderness and created a loving that defied all her doubts. *This* was truth—this unconditional giving and receiving. Everything else paled beside it.

It was daylight when she awoke to find herself the object of Con's inspection. He lay beside her, his head propped on one hand, and at the expression in the azure eyes, a quivering pleasure permeated her body.

'What were you thinking about?' Her voice, husky from sleep, brimmed with anticipation.

'That you're beautiful in the morning, and I'm jealous of your dreams because I can't share them with you.'

'Oh, but you did.' She wound her arms about his neck. 'I dreamed about you all night.'

'Nice dreams?' He nuzzled her, his jaw scraping the soft skin of her throat.

'The best,' she assured him, 'but they don't compare with reality.'

She lay with her hair in careless, shining strands on the pillow, like honey in the sun. 'Ah, Liz,' he sighed against her mouth. 'Some day, I'll write poems about you, compose love songs for you—but not now. Now, I want to show you how much I love you.'

His hands, the vanguard for his eager lips, roamed the length of her, almost spanning the slenderness of her waist, spreading to encompass the soft fullness of her hips. Turning his rapt attention to the tempting length of her thigh, he swept his tongue over the soft, exquisite skin, recalling a promise he'd made to himself weeks earlier that he'd sample the fine silk behind her knees. Indulgence was a rare, intoxicating treat.

Liz knew she felt different, that she saw the world through fresh, enraptured eyes, She had not, however, reckoned on others noticing it too, and was brought to a blushing halt when Janice stopped by her office on the following Monday.

'You want to look over this week's schedule, Liz?' Janice was sifting through the papers in her hands like a professional card sharp, but she snapped to attention when her eyes met Liz's. 'What in the name of sweet sanity's happened to you?' she demanded, consigning the all-important stack of papers to the far corner of a bookcase and bracing her forearms on the desk.

'Nothing ... what do you mean?' Liz aimed for nonchalance, shrugging her shoulders and regarding Janice from large, innocent eyes.

'Why, honey-child, you'se been awakened! You can't hide nuthin' from old Aunt Jemima.'

'Rubbish! And you're too skinny to be Aunt Jemima.'

'Rangy's the word, child, not skinny.' Janice pulled

up a chair and abandoned her frightful southern accent. 'That was a super party you gave on Friday.'

Liz couldn't suppress a smile at the unsubtle shift of topic. Her voice, though, was soft with unconcealed pleasure when she answered. 'It was fun, wasn't it?'

Missing nothing, Janice shot her a narrow, comprehending look. 'It's Con Henderson, isn't it? Old Bedroom Eyes himself? My God!' She clapped a dramatic hand to her brow. 'I would kill for the chance to have at him. That smile, that body, those fabulous lashes! How'd you swing it? I thought you detested him? Why not me, oh Lord?'

It was easy to laugh at Janice's theatrics, and in doing so, to turn aside her probing interest. It was not so simple with Ellen Newman.

Liz usually met her mother for lunch or dinner at least once a week and occasionally for brunch on the weekends. Optimism wasn't part of her parent's nature. What Janice had rejoiced to behold, Ellen regarded with suspicion bordering on alarm.

'You're different, Willie,' she stated nervously. 'Has something happened?'

Liz considered her answer carefully. Unwilling to lie, she deemed it wise to exercise a little judicious caution. Con, in her mother's opinion, was the devil incarnate, hiding his forked tail and cloven hooves under a cloak of corporate respectability. 'I've met someone, Mother. A very nice man.' Ellen's tentative concern blossomed into fear as Liz went on, 'We're been seeing each other off and on for some time.'

'Oh, Willie!' Ellen all but wrung her hands. 'Is it serious?'

Terminal, Liz was tempted to quip, but controlled herself sufficiently to reply off-handedly, 'It's too soon to say.'

'You must be careful, Willie. You know what men can be like. Are you sure you can trust him?'

'I'll find out soon enough. Let's order, Mother. I'm hungry.'

'I couldn't eat a thing! How old is this man?'

Liz stifled a sigh, already regretting her urge to confide in her mother. Ellen had never recovered from the shock of her daughter's first fall from grace, and the passing of time had done nothing to moderate her fears of a repeat performance. 'He's thirty-five.'

'Is he married?'

'Of course not, Mother!'

'Why not, at his age? What's wrong with him?'

'Nothing's wrong. He was married but he's divorced now.'

'Oh. One of those.' Ellen sipped her sherry primly, her lips pursed with disapproval.

'Mother, for heaven's sake, there's nothing wrong with that.'

'It's not a good sign,' Ellen replied darkly. 'Once bitten, twice shy, you know. Can't you find someone nice and single?'

Liz rolled her eyes at her mother's illogical progression of thought. 'At my age, Mother? Hardly. You just said as much, yourself.

It had not been one of their better meetings.

But nothing could dim the radiance of knowing Con loved her. Somehow, in the rush and excitement of Christmas, it was easy to push her deceit to the back of her mind. It was *now* that mattered. Time enough to worry when—or if—he asked her to marry him. If that ever happened, surely she'd be secure enough to be able to tell him anything, even the truth. Thus pragmatic logic ruled the day.

Then, in early January, they drove to Whistler for a day's skiing. It was a day she was to remember; it marked the end of her gilded dreams.

The day which had started out cold with a high overcast turned sullen before noon, and let loose with a full-throated blizzard by three o'clock when the ski lifts closed for the day. It came as no surprise to either of them to learn the road to Vancouver was closed to all traffic because of the risk of landslides along the treacherous coastal highway.

In the midst of the confusion generated by the news, Con took Liz's arm and led her to the car. Locking their skis to the roof rack, he tossed her a conspiratorial wink. 'We're in luck, sweetheart. Unlike most of these poor slobs, we won't have to sleep in the car tonight.'

The condominium to which he took her, located a scant ten minutes from the gondola, was a luxury unit that boasted an open fireplace, a hot tub and a sauna. 'Friends of mine own it,' Con explained, unearthing a key from a window box conveniently situated near the front door. 'They'd want us to use it, I know.'

They sent out for pizza and Con built a fire. Then they ate dinner by candlelight, sitting on the floor before the burning logs, their backs resting on the couch behind them. Later, he tried to talk her into joining him in the hot tub.

'I don't have a swimsuit,' she objected.

'That'll save time.' He accompanied his predatory leer with an insolent pinch to her behind, snugly outlined in close-fitting ski pants. 'The variations on how to have fun in a hot tub are endless and infinitely pleasurable.'

'Are they indeed?' She swatted his impertinent hand. 'You're speaking from experience, I suppose?'

'Sort of.' He pinioned her indignant arms to her sides and let his lips cruise her temples. 'When I was in high school, my brother and I were invited to a pool party. There was one girl there who filled her bikini with the most startling . . . er . . . endowments. We lured her into the pool after dark and stole her top.' His tongue traced her outer ear, his hands rounding her hips with telling effect.

'You brat!' Liz quavered, not sure if she was referring to his wicked past or his masterful present. 'You should be ashamed.'

'It was fun,' he insisted with relish, unrepentant even after all this time. 'We played basketball with it and told her she could have it back if she could catch it.' He leaned back from the waist to observe her reaction, the moment intensifying the close, familiar contact of hip and thigh. 'We were social outcasts for ... the rest of ... the summer ...' His words faded into a husky whisper, his eyes darkening to midnight blue. 'The hot tub,' he breathed, 'can wait.'

Later, in the firelight, he cradled her head on his shoulder. 'Tell me about your life,' he invited. 'You never talk about it. Do you have brothers or sisters?'

'No.' She stirred restlessly. 'I was an only child. Let's try out the hot tub.'

'Weren't you lonely?'

'Very. I wouldn't wish it on anyone.'

'I know how you feel.'

'But you had your brother,' she replied, and realised too late the quicksands closing about her.

'He was killed in Vietnam.' Even after twelve years, Con's voice was hollow with grief. 'I still miss him. He was my best friend.'

I know, my poor darling. I remember the night you found out about his death better than you'll ever realise. 'I'm sorry,' she whispered and hugged him to her. This much, at least, she could offer in perfect truth.

For a moment he relaxed against her, then held her away. 'I'd like to name our first son Steven, after him.'

The world came crashing down on her head. 'I ... son ...?' Her mouth ran dry, along with all the recent joy in her life. Birth control had never been an issue between them; they'd never once discussed it. Obviously, he'd been expecting she'd eventually become pregnant. Oh, God!

'Don't tell me you haven't thought about it?' He caught her lower lip gently in his teeth. 'We'd make beautiful babies together, love.'

Hounded by a misery whose intensity she could never have foreseen, she pushed away from him and reached for her clothes. Covering her nudity from his appreciative gaze, she stepped towards the window and looked out at the thickly falling snow. 'I really haven't considered the possibility,' she replied distantly. What was the point, her breaking heart demanded desolately.

The sweet powdered smell of an infant—her infant—was an achievement so far removed beyond possibility that she'd ceased yearning for it years ago. Too many nights of anguish, lonely sobbing and wishing it weren't so hadn't reversed her condition. They had merely drawn her to the edge of such despair that once, not too many months after her miscarriage, she'd found herself reaching out for a tiny baby strapped into a grocery cart at the supermarket. The look on his mother's face, alarmed and aggressive at the sight of the stranger pawing at her baby, had told Liz quite clearly that her misery and desperation were sliding into something dangerously uncontrolled and fanatical—and that it showed. The mother had sensed a threat in the stranger's attention to her child. Afraid of what her grief might drive her to, Liz had withdrawn to another plane, filled with substitutes: business, success, sophistication.

He didn't miss the familiar withdrawal, though it had been weeks since it had reared up with quite such force. Fear nibbled the edge of his mind. Pulling on his ski pants, he came up behind her and ran a tentative finger down the forbidding rigidity of her spine. 'Hey . . . what did I say wrong?'

She shrugged off his hand. 'Nothing.' What a completely stupid, dishonest response.

He refused to be put off. 'Sweetheart, I'm sorry if I upset you. I'm talking about more than just wanting to prove my manhood, you know. Perhaps I was clumsy, but what I'm really saying is that I want to marry you. I want you to be my wife, the mother of my children.'

She didn't know such pain existed. Her heart seemed to wrench itself free of its moorings and twist into a hard, tight knot of agony. Con's wife, the mother of his children; it was all she'd ever wanted and now could never have.

'Liz?' He turned her to face him, anxiety creasing his blue eyes, furling his lashes into thick crescents. 'Will you marry me?'

Grief choked her throat and erupted as anger. 'Why did you have to spoil things? Why couldn't you leave well enough alone?'

She might have stabbed him, it would have been less cruel. He looked mortally wounded and the urge to cradle his head to her breast and to beg his forgiveness tore at her.

'Are you saying no?'

'Do I have to give an answer right now? Isn't this something we can discuss?' She was flinging up obstacles, desperate to halt the trend of his thoughts. All the joy his proposal should have engendered was engulfed in panic at the approaching juggernaut.

'What's to discuss?' He slumped dejectedly. 'Either you love me enough or you don't.'

'It's not that simple. Don't try to dump guilt on me, Con, just because I want some time. You spring children on me, tag on a marriage proposal as an afterthought, and then get all huffy because I find it rather a lot to deal with at a moment's notice. There's a lot more involved here than just caring.' Impaled by his logic, she was almost shrill in the defence of her position.

'The hell there is!' His eyes, so recently molten with tender passion, were flinty with rage. 'By my reckoning, it's a natural progression from love to marriage. I'd assumed you'd feel the same, which was bloody stupid of me, considering you're still wrapping your tongue around such colourless euphemisms as "caring". I "care" about paying my bills on time, wearing matched socks and getting my hair cut regularly—and you "care" about me. Goddam it, you can't even bring yourself to mention the word "love".'

'But I do love you!' The words burst out.

He laughed without mirth. 'Why do I find that hard to believe, I wonder?'

She stared at him, appalled. 'How could you ever doubt it?'

'Maybe because you've never said so—until now, when you're stuck between a rock and a hard place.'

It was true, she *had* avoided saying those particular words. They were too sacred to be soiled by the deceit she was perpetuating. By leaving them unsaid, it somehow made her dishonesty less repellent. 'Well, if I have reservations about marriage, it has nothing to do with my feelings for you.'

'Then what *is* the problem?'

'I guess it's your assumption that children will be a part of our lives. I'd never given them much thought. I'm thirty years old, Con—past my prime when it comes to having babies.' How smoothly she was covering the truth with evasions—and how shockingly easy it was to let the wicked little lies trip off her tongue. If only she could do it all over again, she'd tell him about their past the very first day he came into her office, admit to her sterility the minute his interest shifted from professional to personal. But to do so now? What possible reason could she offer for withholding the truth this long? Why would any rational person wait three months to raise a subject of such vital concern to both of them?

'Past your prime, my ass! There are thousands of women a lot older than you, having babies.' For a moment he reined in his fury and regarded her intently. 'Is that really the problem? Are you afraid of childbirth, of the responsibility of children?'

Oh, the temptation to spill it all out, and take the consequences. But what if, afterwards, he still persisted with his proposal? How would she discover his true motivation? She could endure his pity even less than his rejection. She hedged again, instead. 'You make me feel like a brood mare. What do you really want—marriage or children?'

'Both. They go together.'

'Is family that important?'

'It's important.'

'Why?'

'Why wouldn't it be? I'm a normal man and I can afford children. Maybe my insecurity's showing, or maybe I'm just an egomaniac but I want sons—and daughters. I want to give my parents the joy of grandchildren. I should think you'd want to do the same for yours. What's wrong with that?'

'Nothing—for you. But what about me? My needs are important, too.'

They were shouting at each other again, tension crackling in the room, and it was ridiculous that so much anger should have displaced the love that had charged the atmosphere only moments earlier. 'Marriage is one thing—I can see sharing it with you; it would be wonderful. But a baby—babies—they take over your life. They don't leave room for anything else.'

May God forgive her. With every word, she was compounding the sins of her untruth. She couldn't bear to meet Con's gaze, couldn't face the revulsion she knew she'd find there. It was enough to hear it in his voice.

'Nothing . . .' He seemed to choke on the words. '*Nothing* prepared me for this! I hadn't figured on this at all.'

'Con, please. My career, my independence, they matter to me.'

He ran a furious hand through his hair. 'I don't believe what I'm hearing. You're telling me that polishing other people's silver and waxing their floors have more meaning for you than a house and children of your own?'

'It's more than that. It's . . . it's everything I've worked to build over the years. Children would be such a . . . disruption.'

'Disruption?' He was flinging on his clothes as he spoke. 'Disruption? How about enrichment?'

'You'd be enough. I'd have everything I need.' She despised the wheedling tone that crept into her voice. It was wrong of her to try to hold him this way. If she couldn't give him what he wanted, she should release him to find someone who could. 'Give me some time,' she begged, and wondered why. Time wouldn't change the unpalatable facts of her sterility.

'Time isn't going to change you from a cold, shallow tease, my darling. You've been stringing me along for months, and I didn't want to know about it. Well, no more.' He hauled on his boots, zipped up his parka. 'Don't wait up for me.'

'Where are you going?' Oh God, he was leaving her . . . again.

'Out.'

'There's a blizzard out there.'

'It's better than what's going on in here.'

She ran to him, her pride in tatters, and clung to his arm. 'No! Don't go—I need you, Con . . .'

He swore at her then, fervently and at length, but it was not his fluent profanity that shocked her. It was the blazing scorn in the glare he directed at her.

'You don't need me, Liz. I'm not sure what you do need, but you don't need me.' He shrugged himself loose of her as effortlessly as if she were a fly, uncaring that she stumbled over a footstool and fell. He strode out, leaving the door swinging on its hinges.

She spent the hours he was gone clutching at improbable solutions, playing a futile game of 'what if', horrified at the extent of her willingness to deceive him further. The possibilities lined up: marry him, agree to raise a family—God knew she would and gladly, if she could—say nothing about her sterility; time would speak for itself. Alternatively, marry him and when he saw how happy just the two of them were, tell him she couldn't have children, and hope by then he wouldn't care anymore. After all, lots of marriages were strengthened by the shared disappointment of child-lessness. Weren't they?

She'd do anything to keep him, she realised with sick

disgust, huddling down beside the fire, her arms wrapped around her drawn-up knees, her face turned to the dying embers—everything except tell him the truth.

Go ahead and tell him, a voice in her head urged. If he really loves you, he'll accept what can't be changed. But she was not, surely, so far sunk in self-gratification that she'd force that choice on him? She'd had a dozen opportunities to tell him everything and chosen not to do so. Sadly, it was now too late.

Funny how things changed. Twelve years ago, she'd been left to cope by herself because of what she'd perceived as his careless indifference towards her. Now, she feared his integrity would bind him to her, when all she wanted was his love. He'd lost nothing over the years; he was still the most vital, attractive man she'd ever known. But with maturity had come responsibility, a heightened sensitivity to others, and the emergence of these qualities added to the original dimensions of his character were almost an extra burden. Ironically, Con at thirty-five was offering her all those things that Con at twenty-three had deprived her of. To tell him the truth now would saddle him with unbearable guilt.

He pushed wide the unlatched door, and stepped into a room that echoed with cold, dark emptiness. Snowflakes clung to his hair, layered his shoulders, but he cared nothing for the melting tracks he left behind as he crossed to the passage leading to the bedroom.

'Liz?' Oh God, she'd gone, driven away by his obstinacy. Had her doubts really been so unreasonable? Did he truly believe the accusations he'd hurled at her? No. He knew what had fired his violent reaction. It was the culmination, tonight, of all the fears he'd harboured over the months of loving her that, ultimately, he could not have her. Like an overindulged child, he'd demanded the moon and thrown a tantrum when it was denied him. When had the word 'compromise' been dropped from his vocabulary? In truth, her doubts about children had some validity, and he didn't give a damn about a family if he couldn't have Liz. *She* was what mattered.

Then, a small movement beside the footstool near the fireplace betrayed her presence and he gave fervent thanks to the Almighty that he'd been afforded a second chance to repair the damage he'd done earlier. She was huddled on the floor like some abandoned, defenceless creature, at the mercy of the whims of an indifferent master.

Covering the distance between them in swift strides, he found her shivering with cold. Kneeling, he tossed kindling and fresh logs on the remains of the fire, stirring the embers to life, then turned and wrapped his arms around her. *Was* it cold that shook her to the bone—or hurt, or sorrow? Remorse rose foul as bile in his throat and uncharacteristic tears stabbed his eyelids.

'I love you, I love you,' he whispered ardently, over and over, rocking her to him, his words muffled by her hair. 'I'm sorry about all I said—it doesn't matter, nothing matters except that I love you.'

His lips grazed her eyelids and tasted the salt of the tears rolling down her cheeks.

'Oh, Con, I love you, too.' The misery on her face, in her voice, lacerated him. He stretched her out on the hearthrug beside him, pressing her to him in an effort to stem the tide of tears, the sobs that continued to shake her.

'Hush, my darling, my love,' he begged, covering her face and neck with desperate little kisses. He couldn't bear what he had done to her, didn't know how to atone. How could he undo the damage, unsay the cruel, destructive words?

His hands worked tirelessly up and down her spine, circling and caressing, striving to drive out the cold of the night and the far more penetrating chill of alienation. And gradually, imperceptibly, out of the shudders of despair grew a trembling of desire that flickered between them like lightning, charging them with reborn passion. The soothing rhythm of his hands altered, their gentle persuasion increasing to a subtle urging, shunning the confining layers that separated them, stripping them away until the silk of her warm curves were pressed to his strong, masculine flesh.

It was like nothing they had ever shared before, a blind searching for comfort, a need to console; their coming together a love laced with sorrow, muted with tenderness, as though to lessen the bitter anger of their fight. Afterwards, Con reached up to the couch behind him and hauled down the pillows and a warm fur throw-over. Bathed in the heat from the fire and the snug solace of the cover, they slept until daylight, limbs entwined, her head at his heart.

CHAPTER TEN

THEY didn't speak of their painful estrangement in the weeks that followed, but it was never quite forgotten. Liz knew they had swept the problem into a corner, knew also that it waited, watchful as a hungry predator, ready to leap out at them, its prey. She feared and hated it and continued her private battle with her outraged conscience.

Con pampered her as though he were trying to coax a dying creature back to life. Her apartment was filled with out-of-season lilac and mimosa and innocent daisies. When Liz and he made love, it was a fevered, urgent thing, as though they both recognised its fragility and were dedicated to its survival.

He showed her in a thousand ways how deeply committed to her he was, and if she could, she would have taken her heart in her hands and given it to him, so desperately did she love him. But, like rot creeping through all their pretences, was her sense of time running out. Yet still she did not tell him the truth. Instead, she played her part in the charade. Only when she was alone did she admit that the spontaneity was gone, the joy sucked away, and knew the fault—and the remedy—lay entirely with her.

March blew in, mild and gentle as the proverbial lamb, purple with crocus, yellow with daffodils. New life abounded all around her, but Liz was depleted of energy, lacklustre and apathetic beside the riotous joy of spring. It was the uncertainty of the outcome with Con that was doing it—or perhaps more accurately, the painful inevitability of it, for how could anything solid and lasting be built on a foundation of misconceptions. Misconceptions! Dear God, her whole existence was revolving around connotations of conception!

The concern of those who loved her—Janice, Sheila, Ellen—seemed merely to exacerbate the listlessness. She was permanently tired, her appetite gone. She went to bed early and awoke drained.

'Go see your doctor,' Janice urged.

'You need a holiday,' Ellen suggested.

'It's probably the 'flu; there's a lot of it about,' Sheila offered.

Con was less vocal about her low spirits, in part because he was frequently out of town on business, and also because she directed all her limited energy to hiding her depression from him. But he sensed something was wrong, and it grieved her that he assumed immediate responsibility for the problem, and tried to atone for whatever sin he had committed with unflagging tenderness and concern for her happiness.

The burden of guilt that she had carried for months was becoming too much to bear. Con wanted the fullest possible relationship with her, not just good sex. And she couldn't give it to him, for all that she loved him. No wonder she felt so debilitated.

Even her own indifference to her health shifted to a stirring of alarm, however, at the persistent malaise that brought her weight to an all-time low. At just over eight stone, she was beginning to look gaunt and food had never been less appetising. It was all she could do to keep down the plainest meal. Her clothes hung on her; everything seemed a size too large, except, strangely, her bra which overflowed with breasts swollen and tender to the touch.

None of it helped to allay the dark suspicions she was beginning to entertain that some horrible, fatal disease had taken hold of her. Yet, her conscience told her, such a fate was perhaps all she deserved. But the day she fainted over her filing cabinet in full view of Janice and Sheila, she was at last persuaded to go to her doctor.

James Swann had overseen her excellent health for more than eight years. A professional to the tips of his skilled fingers, he masked his dismay at her appearance behind his usual cheerful countenance, but she could see that he, too, was concerned.

'You look washed out, Liz,' he commented as he began a thorough physical examination, noting with obvious dismay her pallor and the hollows beneath her eyes. 'You're working too hard at that fancy agency of yours.'

Half an hour later, she faced him across his desk, too wasted to be worried, too miserable to care what he might have to tell her. 'Well, Doctor?'

He made rapid notes in her file, then slapped it shut and formed a steeple of his fingers. 'I'm prescribing iron and vitamins and plenty of rest. I want you to watch your diet, stop skipping meals and be back in my office in a month's time, when I expect you to have put on at least five pounds. You're anaemic, exhausted and underweight—nothing so very unusual, in your condition.'

He paused, a smile tugging at the stern line of his mouth. 'Aren't you the least bit curious to know what I'm talking about, Liz?'

She rested her chin on her hands and gazed back listlessly. 'What's wrong with me?'

'Well, I'm ordering tests to be sure, but if I were a betting man, I'd give you odds on your being pregnant.'

Her spine straightened. 'That's impossible,' she declared flatly. 'I can't have children.'

'It's not impossible at all.' He paused delicately. Not normally a hesitant man, he seemed to be treading with care. 'Why do you feel you can't have children?'

'I'm sterile,' she stated in the same flat monotone. 'You must be mistaken.'

'Where did you get such an idea?' Dr Swann shook his head, puzzled, gesturing to her file. 'There's nothing here to indicate sterility.'

'I had a tubal pregnancy twelve years ago, and lost an ovary.'

'But you've still got the other, and it's functioning perfectly.'

'Oh, I know that, but I also suffered a bad pelvic infection. They told me I'd never be able to have children.'

'A rather rash assumption, I'd say. Sterility following that sort of infection is a possibility, but not necessarily a probability. We can't be absolutely certain until the tests come back, but I'm not really in any doubt about your condition. I'd estimate you're about eight to ten weeks along. When was your last period?'

'I don't keep very good records—they've always been irregular—but I'd guess about the middle of December.'

The middle of December ... oh Lord, if the tests were positive, she had already been pregnant the night Con asked her to marry him. All that misery, all that dreadful subterfuge, had been unnecessary; the image of herself that she'd forced on him—how had he put it? 'cold and shallow'—all for nothing!

Dr Swann consulted the calendar beside him. 'Well, let's see: today's Wednesday ... March seventeenth. I'd predict you'll deliver around the third week in September. Let's make it Monday the twentieth and see how close we come.'

If the tests were positive, there was nothing to keep them apart any longer. Nothing, that was, except for the strain of the past weeks. Their carefully oblique avoidance of anything that might shatter the shell of their relationship had eroded the loving warmth they'd once shared. Could they erase the effects of that strain? They must. They had to!

'How could the doctors at the clinic I attended have made such a mistake?'

'They didn't really. Time has a way of healing all sorts of ills, and there was no way of knowing if the damage from that infection was permanent or not until you tried to conceive. I take it you weren't trying?' The glimmer of a smile lit up his eyes behind their thick lenses.

'Oh!' She clasped her hands prayerfully. 'I never dreamed I could and for such a long time, it didn't really matter.' Her eyes filled with tears, but her voice was light and eager as she spoke. 'But to have it happen now—it's like a miracle. It *is* a miracle.' She turned to him, suddenly anxious. 'When will we know for sure?'

'Tomorrow,' he replied. 'Call my nurse in the afternoon. The results will be in by then.'

Leaving his office, she felt airy as the cloud puffs sailing across the sky, the heavy, wearying burden lifted at last. Now she could tell Con everything. He'd been in Atlanta for the last week, but was expected home by Saturday, and this time, she'd hold back nothing.

It was too gorgeous and rare a day to go back to the agency. Instead, she toured the specialty shops along *Robsonstrasse*, lingering before windows displaying maternity fashions, almost cooing over the baby boutiques. She *was* pregnant, she knew. It was a feeling like no other, not even the first time she'd carried Con's child.

Then, she'd felt so desperately lonely, afraid and unloved, that the baby she was carrying had been a terrifying responsibility she'd barely been able to confront. Maybe fate had been kind after all in relieving her of carrying it to term, for heaven alone knew how she would have supported herself and a child, then.

But not this time. This baby was going to make it.

Before hailing a taxi, she picked up a sack of groceries that would surely have won the approval of Dr Swann: milk, eggs, fruit—the sort of food every unborn baby needed. She was going to play this pregnancy strictly by the book. None of the skimping or self-neglect she'd practiced before. Little Steven was going to get the royal treatment!

'I'd like to call our first son Steven.' Con's words came back to her, no longer a threat, resplendent with hope and love. It was all going to work out; it had to.

Letting herself into her apartment, she regarded it

with pleasurable nostalgia. She'd have to give it up, of course. Con owned a house, and a West End apartment was no place to bring up a baby, but she'd miss its quiet, old-fashioned elegance. There weren't many left like it, but at least she could take her treasured antiques with her. This weekend, she'd start hunting around for an old crib, perhaps a carved rocking chair.

In the bedroom, she shed her working clothes and examined her reflection with wonder, cradling her heavy breasts in her hands, and squinting at her profile in the glass. Was it imagination, or could she detect the first faint hint of a bulge around her middle? She tried to imagine herself, gloriously inflated with impending motherhood, sailing through the stores with that Madonna-like serenity she'd so often envied in other women.

Choosing a rose-pink caftan from the closet, she slipped into its roomy folds, and inserting her hands in the pockets, lifted the fabric away from her abdomen in imitation of advanced pregnancy. It provided a startling but hilarious insight to what she could expect before too much longer. It was difficult to imagine herself too big to see her toes. She'd been slender to the point of thin ever since her last pregnancy.

She did something later that she'd never been able to do with enjoyment before. After a supper of scrambled eggs and dry toast—in deference to her still queasy stomach—she leafed through her graduation yearbook. For the first time, she was able to enjoy the memories it held. She could even smile at the biographical note beside her official portrait.

'Wilhelmina R. E. Newman: member of the debating team, community service co-ordinator, secretary-treasurer of the yearbook committee. Willie's ambition: to travel through Europe and to drop her hated nickname. Remember, Willie, 'A rose by any other name . . .''

Heavens, what a solemn, *worthy* creature she'd been! Small wonder she'd made so little impression on Con, considering the flock of nubile lovelies who'd graduated with her. They'd seemed impossibly glamorous to her then, with their teased hairdos and wired undercup bras. What were they all doing now? Nothing, she was sure, that could equate to the total fulfilment she was experiencing.

She was in the kitchen, heating up milk to make hot chocolate, when the doorbell rang. Heightened intuition lent speed to her step as she hurried to answer it.

'Con!' He was there, tall, elegantly rumpled and glowering adorably. 'What a lovely surprise. When did you get back?'

For once, their roles were reversed. He who, for weeks, had doggedly maintained a cheerful front, appeared anxious and upset. Liz, on the other hand, had miraculously shed the pall of gloom that had been her constant companion for longer than she cared to admit. Even the indignant heavings of her stomach brought a glow of satisfaction to her face tonight.

She reached out to hug him, and found herself held at arm's length instead. 'Are you okay?' He was unusually terse, foregoing the luxury of an embrace.

'Why, yes.' She returned his gaze, her eyes slate grey in the light from the chandelier behind her. The caftan swirled against her, flinging echoes of rose-pink against her skin.

Con closed the door and regarded her searchingly, forced to admit she looked better than she had in weeks. 'Are you sure?'

'Of course.' She smiled at him, a wealth of happiness in her face, but said nothing more. 'She wouldn't confide her news to him until the test showed positive, just in case it was a false alarm. It meant so much to Con to have children. She couldn't raise his hopes and then dash them.

'What did the doctor say?'

'Doctor?' She was dumbfounded. How did he know? *What* did he know?

'You might as well tell me everything.' The blue eyes were stern. 'I called you this afternoon and I know you weren't at work. Sheila told me you'd gone to see your doctor, that you'd fainted in your office. Tell me, Liz.'

So he didn't really know anything! Relief washed over her. 'I'm fine,' she assured him, linking her arms around his waist and pressing her lips to his.

He returned her kiss, but distractedly. 'What did he say?'

'That I'm anaemic and overtired and I have to stop skipping meals.' Oh, the joy of not having to dissemble, the far greater joy of knowing that, after tomorrow, there'd never be any secrets between them again.

'Well, see to it that you pay attention.' Relief was blunting the abrasive edge of his anxiety. He ran his hands down her body, filling them with her slight curves. There was something different about her tonight, a return to that joyous tenderness they'd shared for a brief time around Christmas. It reassured him better than any words that she was indeed well. 'Have you eaten yet?'

'Yes—in fact, I was just making some hot chocolate. Would you like some?'

'Hot chocolate? Whatever happened to that old American standby, coffee?'

'This is better for you.' She rubbed her forehead against his beard, loving the emery scrape of his skin, loving, too, the firm, intimate way he held her to him. 'I'm making it all nice and frothy in the blender.'

He grinned then, looking suddenly younger than his thirty-five years. 'With those tiny marshmallows?'

'Is there any other way?' She peeled herself away from him. 'Hang up your coat and relax. I'll be right back.'

Over the din of the blender, she called to him, 'How was the trip?'

'Pretty good.' He sounded distracted again.

'Will you need to go back?' She missed him dreadfully when he was away. She shrugged at the silence that met her question and poured the foamy mixture into two tall mugs, scattering miniature marshmallows over the top of each. Setting them on a tray beside a plate of cookies, she swirled into the living room. 'Ta-dah! For ... you ...' The words trailed away, the smile freezing on her face as the full import of Con's engrossed silence hit her. Oh God, the yearbook—oh, please, no! Not before she'd had a chance to explain.

When he'd first glanced at the open pages of the book and seen its contents, natural curiosity had impelled him to look closer. Even then, he just might have overlooked the connection, except for the oddity of her girlhood nickname. With a sense of *déjà vu*, he'd flipped to the front of the book and seen the name of the high school they'd both attended, the town where they'd both grown up, and all the pieces fell into place.

There she was, the girl he'd dreamed about for a few brief weeks that unforgettable summer; the girl he'd tried to contact again, after the trip back east to identify Steven, to receive his posthumously awarded medals. One of the things that had sustained Con through all that misery had been the memory of the girl, Willie. She was the quiet one who'd never been part of the 'in' crowd, a loner whom he'd never been close to until the night he'd learned of Steve's death. She'd made it bearable for him. He never saw her again—she had left town by the end of the summer—but he'd never forgotten her sweetness. In the years to come, he had been amazed how often, when things were bad, he'd remember her and wish there'd been some way they could have grown closer.

And the irony of it all was that Liz had reminded him of Willie more than once. Not in looks, really. Willie had hidden herself in drab khakis and browns as though she were trying to ensure the world wouldn't notice her. His Liz epitomised elegant fashion, was always tastefully and impeccably turned out. But, when he looked closer at the portrait, he could see the resemblance. Even allowing for the protective curtains of hair that draped Willie's face, there was no hiding the finely chiselled bone structure; even more revealing was the air of reserve in her eyes, holding her apart from the rest of the world as much in adolescence as it did in adult life.

He glanced up, suddenly aware that she was in the room again and that she'd started to speak. Any doubts he might have entertained about what he had just discovered were swept aside by the look of guilty horror on Liz's face.

It was as if she'd been planted at that spot just inside the living room, and had promptly put down deep, enduring roots. Nothing short of a major earthquake could have moved her—except for Con.

Lifting incredulous eyes to hers, he rose and relieved her of the tray, placing it with exaggerated care on the coffee table. Straightening again, he resumed his perusal of her, stalking around to view her from different angles while she stood, mute with humiliation and apprehension, fighting to keep down her half-digested supper.

At last he spoke. 'You're Willie.' She flinched at his words, but his voice was surprisingly soft and non-accusatory.

He lifted one of her hands and balanced it on his palm as though he were about to lead her in a formal minuet. 'Willie Newman—Liz Newman!' The wonder in his tone confused her. He scarcely sounded like a man betrayed; rather, he appeared mildly ecstatic. 'Why didn't I spot it sooner? It's so obvious, now that I know.'

'I was——'

'Why didn't you——?'

They spoke together, their simultaneous outbursts freeing her from the catalepsy that had gripped her. 'I was going to tell you tonight, Con. That's one reason I had the annual out.'

'Do you know how often I've thought about you over the years? How often I've wondered what happened to you? Why didn't you tell me who you were at the beginning?'

'I *am* Liz Newman. I dropped Willie years ago.'

'You know what I mean. Why all the secrecy?'

She trembled, a frail leaf in the grip of a violent inner storm. 'I was afraid.'

'Of what?' He caught both her hands lightly and stepped back to examine her more fully.

'Of you.'

'Of me? Sweetheart, why?'

'I thought it would change how you felt about me. I thought you'd despise me.'

'Why on earth would I do that? What reason would I have?'

She pulled her hands free and sat down on the couch, suddenly fearful her legs might not be equal to supporting her. The after-effects of shock were taking effect; all at once, she felt light-headed. 'Oh-h . . .' It was a plea for understanding, a softly uttered gasp of resignation.

'Tell me, Liz. Why would I despise you?'

'I was so . . . different from the others. You must have had a real laugh about me after . . . after we . . .' Even now, she couldn't bring herself to say the words.

'We made love on the beach one summer night, and it was so bloody fantastic, we did it again and again in that shelter under the trees. I was pretty drunk at first, and had a hell of a head the next day, but I remember enough to know that. You needn't pussyfoot around the subject, Liz. I know perfectly well what we did. What I don't understand is why I never saw you again, or why, when we met years later, you pretended we were strangers.'

'I already told you—I didn't think I was your type. I thought you'd laugh at me. I was rather pathetic, after all.'

'You were the most caring girl I'd ever been with. I wanted to die that night, and you turned everything around for me; you made me believe I could face the future. It never occurred to me to laugh at you. You must have had a pretty low opinion of me to think that.'

'I loved you. I've never loved anyone else. I remember the day I first saw you, stuffing baskets in the gym at Cannon River High. I would have kissed your boots if you'd let me. As it was, you didn't know I existed.'

He spread his hands. 'What can I say? I *don't* remember that. But I do remember coming home from college and seeing you about town. Everyone called you Willie. I didn't know your surname, but I knew who you were. And I knew who you were that night, too. It was a very special night for me.'

'Then why didn't you call me again?'

'Honey, I did. Oh, not right away. The next day, my father and I flew back east to pick up ... Steve ... and to receive a special citation on his behalf. We had to identify him, too.' A shadow passed over his face, and he winced as he spoke. 'It was brutal. We were gone several days, and then brought Steve home. My mom didn't go with us—she couldn't handle that part of things. It was bad enough for her at the funeral. But ...' He shook off the painful memories determinedly. 'After it was all over, I 'phoned your house. Your mother said you weren't there. I 'phoned again, a couple of times, and you were never home. She wasn't very encouraging, and eventually I went off to basketball training camp for a month without getting hold of you. Then, when I came home, I stopped by your house, and she told me you'd left town. I practically crawled down the driveway afterwards. She made me feel about as welcome as a termite.'

Oh, Mother! What have you done to my life in your neurotic effort to protect me from the things you decided weren't good for me? Liz passed a weary hand over her face. 'I never knew.'

'I assumed you'd gone off to college, or that there

was someone special in your life, and that she didn't want me lousing things up for you. I never tried again.'

She could have wept. All that pain for nothing! 'If only I'd known.'

'We've wasted a lot of time, but maybe it's for the best. I don't know if I was ready to make a lasting commitment then. You were special, but I'd be lying if I said I was in love with you. I didn't know you—but I wanted to.'

'And now?'

He slid on to the cushions beside her and took her in his arms. 'You know how I feel now.' His lips lingered lightly on hers, brushing softly back and forth, his hands persuading her to him. 'Lust and love have finally caught up with each other!' His kiss deepened as his hands began a languid tour of her body that left her quivering in every nerve. 'Does it matter that I took so long?' He bent his head and, with his mouth, pushed aside the loose opening of the caftan, allowing his tongue to trespass in easy familiarity along her collarbone.

She was tempted, sorely tempted, to postpone the epilogue to their first romance. It was difficult to ignore Con's magical hands sliding over the smooth skin of her arms beneath the wide sleeves, kneading the ripe swell of her breasts, seeking to awaken the nipples that blossomed so readily at his touch.

Did he notice any difference, she wonderd. Could he feel the extra fullness as her body prepared itself to nurture his son? The joy of today banished the pain of yesterday. No, it didn't matter that it had taken him twelve years. Nothing mattered any more; she was carrying his child again, and that made everything right. But . . .

Unwillingly, she pulled back from him. 'There's more,' she told him.

His eyes were smouldering with passion. 'Can't it wait? I've been gone a week. Don't you know it's bad for a man to have his appetites thwarted this way?' He applied himself to the pleasure of seduction again, one hand cupping her hip, the other taking her hand and pressing it to the evidence of his unashamed desire.

Resolve wavered . . . then overcame temptation as she recalled her earlier promise to herself that tonight she would tell all. The worst was over. He knew she was Willie and still he wanted her. The truth had done nothing to dim his love. 'No, Con. It can't wait.'

Resigned, he sat back and regarded her menancingly. 'Okay, lady, But if I suffer irreversible damage as a result of this, I shall hold you responsible.'

His comment, harmless and teasing, was a dramatic reminder of the cost to her of their one-night affair twelve years ago. 'I left Cannon River because I was pregnant,' she told him, her voice carefully neutral. She might have been delivering the weather forecast.

He was suddenly still, his whole body tense with some fierce emotion that held him rigid. 'With my child?' His tone, as precisely controlled as hers, belonged to a stranger.

'Yes.'

'Go on.'

'I lost the baby.'

'Did you have an abortion?' The question shattered the air between them.

'No! I had a miscarriage—a tubal pregnancy, actually, and I lost an ovary. Do you remember when you asked me about my scar?'

'I remember very well.' His voice was iron hard and her fluttering apprehension threatened to spill into panic. Why was this so hard for him to accept, when the rest had seemed so easy?

'Please don't be angry. It wasn't my fault, or yours.' She looked at him beseechingly. 'Sometimes, pregnancies just don't work out, no matter how much you may want them to.'

'But it *was* my child, too—or didn't that matter to you?'

'Yes, it mattered, but I didn't know you cared. You

hadn't followed up on that night; I thought it had meant nothing to you.'

'But my child would have!' His fury erupted in a roar. 'Goddam you, Liz. Where do you get off deciding not to tell me about that?'

'You already said you weren't in love with me then. Why should I have told you?'

'Because I had a right to know! I may not have thought I was ready for marriage, but if I'd known you were pregnant, I might have seen things differently.'

'I didn't want you under those terms——'

'You had no right to keep it from me! Damn you, you had no right!'

It was like the night at Whistler all over again. Black rage had erupted in sudden force and swept away all the tenderness and desire. 'It would have made no difference. The pregnancy could never have gone to term.'

'That's not an excuse. It doesn't make what you did right.' He paced agitatedly back and forth, casting furious glances at her. 'What else haven't you told me?'

Unable to meet his gaze, she peered down at her hands, twisted together in her lap, the skin over her knuckles gleaming whitely. 'Nothing . . .' she mumbled.

His clearly enunciated expletive shocked and angered her. She'd opened the closet to expose the skeleton and what happened? Meek, timid little Willie leaped out and took over again! Meeting his black, disbelieving glare head on, she squared her shoulders. 'Don't use that language on me. I'm not one of your hired lumber-jacks.'

'You're a liar.' His words ricocheted around the room, stunning her with their cruelty.

'And you're a bastard. But since you're so obsessed with every last detail, I'll give you the rest of the story. Bearing in mind how royally ticked off you are at the way I treated you, I shall take considerable pleasure in letting you know the result of our ill-fated one-night stand.'

He flinched at her icy assessment, but made no effort to interrupt.

'My mother decided that Cannon River was too small a town for my "condition" to pass without undue comment. My mother, you see, had very rigid ideas on what constituted proper behaviour, and illegitimate pregnancies didn't make her list. So, since I'd taken a summer job with your father's firm, I asked for a transfer to their Vancouver office. I was given a position as a dogsbody, performing various menial office tasks—making coffee for the bosses and all that sort of thing. I had no saleable skills, of course—my education had come to a rather sudden halt—and I was paid a pittance. Medical care was a luxury I had to forego, since the company I worked for offered no insurance to new employees. In itself, that made no difference to the outcome of the pregnancy, but I might, had I been able to afford proper care, have been spared the pelvic infection that followed.'

'A totally unnecessary complication if you'd been honest with me. At the very least, I could have paid your expenses.' Con flung the words at her, furious that she'd endangered her health because she was too proud to come to him.

'The very least wasn't what I needed, Con. I was eighteen and scared witless. My mother was still in Cannon River, practically apoplectic, and I had no one else to turn to. You seemed to have lost interest as quickly as you'd found it and I was damned if I was going to force a confrontation, with your whole family in mourning. I did the best I could.'

'And wound up with nothing!'

'Less than nothing—I wound up possibly sterile and unemployed. When I needed the work the most, Henderson's fired me because I'd had too much time off. That's when I turned to house-cleaning for a living.'

'Sterile?' He was ashen, suddenly, all his rage subsiding into an appalled whisper.

'*Possibly* sterile. At the time, I was more concerned with keeping a roof over my head and——'

'*Sterile?*' His eyes, piercingly blue, were wide with shock.

'Is that all that's registered with you? Your father's company fired me because I had to take time off from work. I was practically destitute. I lived at the poverty line for over a year!'

'It was your own fault. None of that need have happened if you'd come to me.'

His callous dismissal of her agony inflamed her. Springing to her feet, she drew back her hand, longing to feel the punishing sting of her palm across his cheek, but he forestalled her. Gripping her wrist in fingers that cared nothing for her delicate frame or the bruising that would darken her skin tomorrow, he impaled her in a gaze as bleak and forbidding as a Siberian winter.

'Do you want to now what finally finished off my marriage?' He ground out the words with vicious clarity. 'Eva became pregnant and without consulting me, she decided to have an abortion. Motherhood was not to her taste; she simply couldn't be bothered with the inconvenience, the *distortion* of pregnancy. I was told after the fact. My own child was disposed of and I didn't even know it had been conceived.'

Liz stared at him in growing horror. This was a stranger, full of deadly intent, consumed with bitterness for the women who'd cheated him of fatherhood. 'It wasn't the same . . .' she faltered.

'It was *exactly* the same.' He dropped her wrist as if it were contaminated. '*Exactly.* You denied me the right to know my own child.'

'No, Con!' Huge, terrified sobs convulsed her. 'I didn't end the pregnancy. It was just one of those things that happen sometimes. I wanted my baby.'

'I'd have wanted him, too. But if he'd survived, I'd never have known him. I could have had an eleven-year-old child walking around town and passed him on the street without knowing him.'

She collapsed on the couch, unable to deny the truth of his allegations. 'I didn't know you'd care.'

'It would have been relatively simple to find out.' Turning on his heel, he strode out of the room, and her heartbeat hung in abeyance as she waited fearfully for the sound of the front door closing behind him. Instead, from the kitchen, came the clink of ice and in a moment Con returned, a tumbler of Scotch in his hand.

Ignoring her, he marched over to the window and stared out. 'So, where do we go from here? What's left of our relationship?'

'I love you.' It was so easy to say the words, now that it was too late.

He laughed, a bitter, tearing sound. 'I love you, too, but it isn't enough, is it?'

'What do you mean?' Her heartbeat, so recently atrophied with fear, was galvanised by pure terror.

'Trust, Liz.' He swung round to face her and raised his glass in a mocking salute. 'The word I've been trying to define for you all along. There has to be trust—and with us, there isn't. I suppose, given time, I could accept what you did twelve years ago. I suppose you had your reasons—or thought you did. But I can't swallow the stunt you've been pulling for the last six months. You could have explained all this at Whistler. Instead, you let me accuse you of being cold and shallow, then left me to wallow in guilt when my insensitivity almost destroyed you. You've been playing games with me all along.'

He drained his glass. 'I'm not sure I can trust you, and it's clear you don't trust me. How can we possibly build anything on that?'

She could say: We must. I'm pregnant with your child again. She could, but she wouldn't. He'd force the relationship to work then, and she didn't want him on those terms. If 'possibly sterile' Liz wasn't enough, pregnant Liz wasn't either.

'Perhaps we can't.' Defeat, disappointment, were an unbearable weight. She stared at the fireplace, knowing how impossible it was to meet his fiercely blue, forthright stare. 'But I'd like to try.'

She thought he wasn't going to answer. The silence between them stretched, taut as a bowstring. All the airy lightness had fled her body, leaving it heavy with despair.

'I came home early from Atlanta because I missed you so much. I wish I'd stayed away.'

His anger had filtered away, to be replaced by such utter weariness and dejection that she was assailed with pain at the hurt she had dealt him. 'Con . . .' She turned imploringly towards him.

'I'm going before I say or do something I'll really regret. I need time to sort everything out. I think you do, too. You know what I'm looking for, but I'm not sure what it is you want, or if you even know yourself.'

With his thumb and middle finger, he pinched the bridge of his nose, then ran his hand down over his face as though to wipe off the desolation engraved on it. 'I'm willing to give a lot to a relationship, but I'll ask a lot, too. I don't know if you're capable of fulfilling that need. I won't put up with this holding back, Liz, not any more. I'm all through with half measures, which is what I was willing to settle for following that fiasco at Whistler. If we make it through this and you hold out on me one more time, we're finished. You can count on it.'

He placed his glass on the tray beside the cooling mugs of chocolate, then walked quietly across the room and out the door. No kiss, no hug, no touch of the hand. Not a single breath of life to stir the ashes of her despair. He walked out as if she weren't there, leaving her with the secret knowledge that, even in the face of this final ultimatum, she was defying him, hoarding the one piece of news that might possibly succeed in mending the rift in their relationship.

CHAPTER ELEVEN

HE'LL call, she told herself. He'll get over it, like he did before, at Whistler. And then, he'll 'phone, or come over, and we'll talk, quietly and reasonably, and I'll make him understand.

But he didn't call, not that night or the next day. Anxiety probed her mind, dispelling rational thought, leaving dark and empty corners where panic multiplied. How long before he made up his mind? What if he never came back?

On the surface, she was herself, directing agency affairs with cool efficiency, brushing aside solicitous enquiries about her fainting spell of the day before.

'Nothing to worry about,' she told Janice and Sheila. 'I've got to stop missing meals, that's all.'

At three o'clock in the afternoon, she dialled Dr Swann's office and spoke to his nurse. 'It's Liz Newman. Are the results of my pregnancy test in yet?'

'Hold on and let me check. All the lab reports are here someplace.' There was the sound of shuffling papers, a 'phone ringing on another line, the montonous bell tone indigenous to medical buildings pinging at regular intervals. 'The test results are positive, Ms Newman. Congratulations.'

'Thanks.' Years of practice fortified her, enabling her to respond in a suitably controlled fashion, to arrange her next appointment, to thank the voice on the other end of the 'phone. Only after she hung up did the banked fires of joy spring alive in her face, banishing the chill of Con's displeasure. No matter what else happened, she was going to have a baby.

Optimism flourished. If he hasn't 'phoned by eight tonight, I'll call him, she decided. I'll convince him, somehow, that we can work things out. Then, I'll tell him, and it will be wonderful.

She tried not to watch the clock, not to stare hypnotically at the silent telephone, willing it to ring. After dinner, she settled down on the couch with her feet up and aimed the remote control switch at the television, flipping past old movies and syndicated reruns, looking for something to engross her, anything to pass the time.

Her attention was caught first by the name, then by the serious face of the announcer, his sombre tone freezing her finger to hold the local news channel in focus.

'. . . the Henderson mill in northern B.C. Three men are dead, and four still missing in what appears to be a tragedy triggered by managerial differences. Peter Morrison and our news crew are at the site with this updated report.'

The camera angle widened to show a second monitor behind the newscaster, then zeroed in on the smaller picture until it filled the home screens. At some point, Liz had swung her feet to the floor and was leaning forward, attention riveted on the programme.

Morrison appeared, zippered to the chin in a down parka, his breath puffing out in clouds of condensation as he spoke into a hand-held microphone. In the background, two helicopters prepared for take-off.

'A recovery boiler exploded this morning at a Henderson Industries mill here in this remote corner of the province. Three men are dead and four still unaccounted for and the question everyone is asking is: Why?

'The millworkers' mood is ugly. They feel victimised by a managerial dispute which has claimed the lives of some of their colleagues and which, if it goes unchecked, could pose a threat to others.'

The camera shifted to another shot and a soft gasp escaped Liz's lips as Con, in hard hat and overalls, his face lined with weariness, filled her television screen.

The report ran for a further five minutes, exposing the cause of the tragedy: the operations manager refusing to shut down his mill for routine servicing because delivery had not been made on spare parts; the steam plant superintendent denying responsibility because he'd warned his colleague of the potential danger; and the resultant explosion that left widows and children to mourn their men.

Con was terse and troubled. Henderson Industries would initiate a thorough investigation. The company would shoulder the final responsibility for the loss of life and the injuries. He would not, be affirmed, permit a repeat of the circumstances which had brought about this tragedy. Henderson Industries was more concerned with the well-being of its employees than it was in the uninterrupted running of its mill.

Oh Con! Her heart went out to him. This, on top of last night, was too much. Guilt nagged at her again. There was nothing she could have done to prevent the mill tragedy, but she could have spared him last night's agony by admitting to the truth months before. She could have sent him away happy by telling him she was pregnant again and that, this time, he would share every moment with her.

But I wasn't sure last night, she defended herself.

You were holding out on him, punishing him, her conscience retorted. You wouldn't have told him even if you had been sure.

She bowed her head, ashamed. It was true.

She had to come to terms with herself, she knew. It could be several days until Con came home, but when he did, she must have ironed out all the wrinkles in her mind. He'd been right. She *did* need to examine her priorities. And if scoring off him was still necessary to bolster her sense of confidence or control, then she should let him go. They couldn't build a future on that.

She was amazed, when she really examined the reasons for her behaviour, at how much unresolved anger still lingered. She thought it had dissipated months ago, but there were still pockets of it persisting, and they had to be faced and dealt with.

And the first, she decided, snapping off the TV and lifting the 'phone off its cradle, was to deal with Ellen. 'Mother, are you free for lunch tomorrow?'

Ellen's affront at her daughter's brusque question showed in her fluttering, primly proper response. 'Oh! Hello, Willie. How nice to hear from you. *How are you?*' Manners, Wilhelmina! came the unspoken reprimand. Manners before all else.

'I'm fine. What about tomorrow?'

There was a tiny pause, enough to convey Ellen's continued disapproval of the tenor of the conversation. 'I'm afraid tomorrow's out, dear. In fact, I'm busy right through the weekend. Can it wait until Monday?'

No. Monday was too far away. Con would be back by then and she wanted to face him with a clean slate. 'How about dinner tomorrow?'

'Yes, I could manage that, but you're usually busy on Friday nights. Why aren't you seeing that friend of yours?' Ellen's tone suggested the Boston Strangler would have made a more suitable companion than the man her daughter had settled for, and Liz smiled grimly. It was time to set her mother straight, too. Long past time, in fact.

'Come here for dinner.' The invitation emerged as a near-command. A restaurant would be far too public a place for what she had in mind to discuss. 'About six-thirty?'

The television was tuned to the same news channel when Ellen arrived the next evening.

'I want to find out what's happening in that boiler explosion up north,' Liz explained, giving her mother a hug and settling her in a chair beside the fire. 'Dinner will be about half an hour, so we have time for a drink.' She poured sherry for her mother and tonic and lime for herself. 'I'll just check on things in the kitchen, then we can relax.'

She had it all planned, knew just how she was going to broach the subject of Con, exactly how she'd handle her mother's predictable objections. Tossing the salad, she rehearsed her opening speech. You remember Con Henderson, don't you, Mother?

'Your news report's on, Willie.'

'Oh!' Sliding crêpes stuffed with crab and asparagus into the oven, she hurried through to the living room in time to hear the dire announcement.

'Trouble continue to stalk Henderson Industries. After yesterday's explosion which took the lives of four men, another tragedy is feared to have taken place . . .'

Four lives? That meant another man had died since yesterday. Liz perched on the arm of the couch, her brow furrowed with concern. Another body found? Or an injured man lost?

'. . . Air and sea search planes are combing the area, but no wreckage has been sighted as yet. Conroy Henderson, president of the Canadian branch of the multi-million dollar international forest products concern, is the only son of Joshua Henderson, founder of the company. A family spokesman declined comment on the plane's disappearance.'

A rectangle filled with a still-shot of Con, smiling into the camera, loomed over the announcer's right shoulder, then faded as a fresh topic of news was introduced. The impersonal voice continued its task, keeping the people informed, while Liz fought a losing battle to free herself from the invisible molasses that gummed up her mind and reduced her body movements to a slow, enfeebled groping of arms and legs. She had to stop the announcer and make him go back; she didn't understand what he was saying. Where was Con?

'Con Henderson's gone missing!' her mother exclaimed in appalled fascination. 'Did you hear, Willie?'

A guttural protest escaped from Liz's throat, drawing Ellen's attention away from the television. 'Willie!'

'I have to go, Mother . . .' It was so inordinately difficult to focus, to discipline her errant limbs. She was flailing about like a skid row wino, lurching from one piece of furniture to the other, and the distances between them were *so* vast.

'You're ill, Willie. Let me help you.' Ellen hurried to take her arm and endeavoured to steer her towards the bathroom.

Runnels of tears, born of frustration and terror, suddenly coursed down Liz's cheeks. 'I could 'phone,' she wailed. 'Couldn't I?' She turned, a child again, looking to her parent for comfort and guidance.

'Yes ...' Ellen murmured uncertainly, completely undone by her daughter's emotional outburst. She hadn't seen her cry in years, not since ... Oh, good heavens! The news report. An awful premonition seized her. 'Willie? Is this about Con Henderson?'

But Liz shook her off and turned blindly for the telephone. It rang before she could reach it, and she stumbled to silence it. 'Con? Con?'

A man's voice came over the line, grave but calm. 'Liz, this is Sam Fiedler. Have you heard the news?'

'What's happened, Sam? Tell me where Con is. I need to go to him.'

Beside her, Ellen sagged, no longer spry and elegant, but shrunken suddenly, and old.

'His plane hasn't checked in, Liz, but there's no cause for panic.'

'Tell me.' The tears were drying on her face and her voice was unnaturally calm, her body still as death.

Sam did his best. 'He left the mill site this afternoon in a company float plane, and we haven't had contact with him since. A storm blew in over the north coast, a real blizzard, I gather. He probably changed his flight plan—he may be on the Island or he could be holed up waiting out the storm in one of the fjords. I'm sure we'll hear tomorrow.'

'Was he alone?'

'No. He has one of our best pilots with him—a man who knows the area like the back of his hand. They'll be all right, I'm sure.'

'What shall I do?' It was the plaintive cry of a lost child.

'There's nothing you can do. Stay by the 'phone and I'll be in touch the minute I hear anything. But Liz . . .?' She heard his indrawn breath and braced herself for more. 'Do yourself a favour and don't listen to the media reports, please. Call *me* if you want to know anything, okay?'

'Okay.'

'One thing more. Is there someone I can contact to stay with you tonight?'

'My mother's here, Sam.' Ellen, she realised, was stroking her forearm in gentle, soothing reassurance, and at her daughter's words, the other woman took the receiver and spoke firmly into it.

'This is Mrs Newman. How may I help my daughter?'

'Stay with her, ma'am. It's going to be a long night and she shouldn't be alone.'

'Put your mind at rest, young man. I'll be here as long as she needs me.'

It was quite remarkable, Liz decided with the detachment that separates a person from pain or horror too great to be borne, how some people thrived on disaster. Look at Ellen, strong and certain for the first time in years. Somehow she had bundled Liz in a quilt and settled her on the couch, adjusting pillows and cushions to give her comfort. She had made hot milk with sugar and a medicinal dose of brandy, and was urging it on her daughter with all the kindly insistence one would bestow on an invalid.

'Drink it down, darling. It'll help you feel better.'

'It won't help the baby,' Liz told her forlornly, 'and it won't do anything for me, either.'

'Baby?' Ellen seated herself beside Liz and cupped her cheek. 'What do you mean?'

'I'm going to have a baby, Mother.'

'Con's?'

'Yes. I thought I couldn't have any more children. Do you remember? But I just found out yesterday that I'm pregnant again.'

'Then we must take special care of you until Con gets home.'

Ellen's calm acceptance penetrated Liz's misery more thoroughly than any scandalised hysteria. Everyone, it seemed, had changed since Cannon River. Liz well remembered her mother's frenzied efforts to shunt her out of town as quickly as possible, before she began 'to show'. Yet, the way she was accepting the news the second time around, one would think her impervious to shock or upset.

'Is that all you're going to say?' she asked in disbelief.

'I want to see you happy. If being with Con and having his baby is what you want, then I want it, too.'

Liz propped herself up one one elbow. 'Mother, did Con ever try to get in touch with me, that summer . . . that time his brother died and I . . .'

'When you were pregnant before? Yes, he did, more than once. I sent him away and never told you.'

The admission completely defeated Liz. It wasn't so much that she'd disbelieved Con's story as that she'd expected far greater resistance from her mother. All her anticipated indignation seeped away, leaving only the mystery of this strangely subdued woman. 'Why, Mother?'

It was as if, in the face of impending sorrow and loss, Ellen was gathering her meagre courage in her two hands and forcing herself to confront her own culpability.

'It wasn't so much him,' she began, and turned eyes of the same blue-grey intensity as Liz's towards the fire. 'It was what I knew—or thought I knew—about all men. They're so . . . removed, somehow. They don't give like women.'

'Con loves me, Mother, and I may have lost him without his ever knowing just how much I love him. He may die without knowing I'm carrying his child, because I didn't trust him enough to tell him. What's wrong with us that we're so suspicious of other people's motives?'

Ellen turned her grave regard on her daughter. 'It's not other people we mistrust, Willie. It's men—and I've encouraged you to be suspicious since you were old enough to understand, because I let what happened to me colour all my thoughts. God help me, I passed it on to you, too, without once considering that you had a right to your own mistakes—your own life.'

'What are you trying to tell me?' Liz sank back against the pillows. 'You and Daddy had an idyllic marriage. There was never any other man for you. How can you be so bitter?'

'My marriage was never idyllic, Willie, because I . . . we . . .' Ellen turned away again briefly, then faced Liz squarely. 'Your father and I were never married.'

It seemed to Liz that her jaw dropped in direct proportion to the degree that her eyes widened. 'You mean I was . . .?'

'Born out of wedlock.' The words, old-fashioned and uttered with such self-condemnation, were almost an obscenity on her mother's lips. 'I came from a strict New England family that revered virtue above all else. My father was a minister; we never had much money—I suppose "poor as church mice" would have described us perfectly—but he was highly regarded in the community. I was plain and dull and devoted to good works—a dreadful bore, now that I come to think about it. Can you believe that at thirty-two, I'd never had a date?

'Then, one Sunday, Clifford Pearce, the son of one of the town's leading families, came home. He was an officer in the army and he'd remained in Europe after the war. I was, as we used to say then, quite smitten.'

'My father?'

'Yes.'

'What was he like?'

'Oh, my dear, he was as handsome and carefree as

the devil himself—and almost as unprincipled. He taught me that virtue isn't its own reward—it doesn't amount to a hill of beans unless you squander it on someone of your own class. I was *not* of his class!

'I don't know why he pursued me. Heaven knows, all the single girls in town and probably half the married women, too, would have been glad to be seen with him. But for some reason, he chose me—the plainest of them all.'

A spasm clutched briefly at Liz's heart at the pain in her mother's eyes. She knew exactly how she'd felt. Like mother, like daughter!

'Well, he seduced me,' Ellen stated briskly. 'I made it painfully easy for him. We had an affair that lasted right into the new year. He gave me silk stockings with black seams for Christmas, I remember. I hid them from my father.

'When I told Clifford I was pregnant, he laughed at me, called me his silly little virgin. Said he wasn't ready for fatherhood, that he knew a place I could go—a doctor. He wanted me to have an illegal abortion. When he saw how—devastated—I was at the idea, he said he'd stick by me, that we'd work things out. But he didn't. He went back to Europe and I never saw him again. He married a French girl and was killed in a car accident in the Pyrenees a month before you were born.

'You always had his picture by your bed.' Liz had spent hours as a child, examining the photograph of the handsome, smiling face until she knew its every feature by heart.

'All part of the charade. And, he was my only love, dear. I never forgot him. That picture—and you—are all I have to remind me of him.'

'What happened after he left?'

'Well, you can't hide a pregnancy for long, you know, especially not in a small town. I had to tell my father, and he and my aunts—my mother died when I was eight—well, they went to his family and presented me like a piece of evidence. Oh, the humiliation of it all!

His family tried to do the decent thing, by their standards. They offered me money, enough to go away and raise my child without bringing disgrace on their name. To my lasting regret, I refused it. It was a gesture I couldn't afford, though my pride felt better for it at the time. But later, I wished I'd thought less of myself and more about you. Money could have made life a lot more comfortable for you.'

'We always had enough for the things that mattered.'

'Perhaps. Anyhow, Clifford and I were worlds apart, and it was plain there would never have been a place for me in his life. I had to leave New England, of course. My family were disgraced and it seemed the least I could do to take myself away. So I came west and you were born in Seattle; then, when you were still a baby, we moved to Cannon River. Everyone thought I was a respectable widow and you were safe from the stigma of your illegitimacy.'

'Well, when you became involved with Con—oh Willie, I was so afraid for you! You were a lovely girl, far prettier than I'd been, and I'd tried to raise you as a lady. Appearances, I'd discovered, counted for a lot, and I wanted to protect you from the sort of discrimination I'd suffered. But, underneath, we were nobody. And the Hendersons—they owned the town we lived in. I was so sure you'd be ruined, as I was. So sure all Con wanted was a fling, and that then, you'd be left with no reputation.'

'Then I became pregnant by Con and it was like the re-run of an old nightmare.' Liz leaned forward and put her arms around her mother. 'You should have told me.'

'I was terrified for you, certain that Con would eventually tire of you. But I was thinking of me, too, and that was wrong. I didn't realise until today how wrong. When two people belong together, no one has the right to come between them. You and Con found each other again, for all my interference. I only hope I'll

have the chance to tell him how sorry I am for keeping
you apart before.'

For a little while, she'd been able to immerse herself
in her mother's story, but Ellen's words, with their
undertones of doom, were a bleak reminder of the
present. 'He has to be safe, Mother. He'll want this
baby so badly.'

'Of course he's safe.' It was back, that strength she'd
never before associated with her mother. 'He has
everything to live for.'

'He doesn't know I'm pregnant. I didn't tell him. We
had a terrible fight the last time I saw him.' The tears
held in check for almost two hours, slid down her face
again. 'He was so angry at me for not having told him
about the other pregnancy.'

'He loves you and you love him. I know, now, that
that's what matters. If you have that, you can work
everything else out. You'll see.'

Liz didn't think the night would pass, didn't believe
she could sleep, but she did, and awoke to a fresh day
that brought no news of Con.

'We'll find him,' Sam insisted. 'The storm's easing
off and once the visibility improves, the search planes
will be out again and they'll spot him. He's got
emergency supplies to last him a week and he's
tough.'

The comfort of his words soon died, though, in the
face of the slow-moving hours with no further word.
Once, she ignored Sam's advice and tuned into the
televised news.

'The search for Conroy Henderson and his pilot goes
on,' the voice proclaimed, 'but bad weather and rugged
terrain are feared to have claimed two more lives in the
on-going tragedy at the Henderson——'

'That ...' Ellen, reappearing silently from some
kitchen task, reached over Liz's shoulder and pressed
the off switch, '. . . is precisely the sort of speculation we
don't need. Mr Fiedler has the most current news. Shall
I 'phone him?'

'I guess not. He said he'd call us if he heard.'

The day dragged, seeming to linger twice over each passing minute. For all her efforts to remain calm and protect her baby from stress, Liz felt the tension accumulating in her neck, the small of her back, behind her eyes.

Ellen's attempts to divert her became a source of unbearable irritation, aggravated by the guilt of her ingratitude. She knew her mother was trying to help, rushing to forestall her every need, hovering, an impotent guardian angel, at her shoulder; knew, too, that in performing little acts of loving kindness, Ellen was trying to atone for her past omissions.

But when the third day dawned without any word, Liz asked her mother to go home.

'I need to be alone.' She tried to be kind, tried not to rush to hold open the door.

'What if you need something, Willie? I hate to leave you.'

'If I need you, I'll call. Please, Mother.'

She had to be by herself to confront what the last few days had exposed. When Ellen was gone, she wandered through the rooms of the apartment, seeking the solace they had so reliably offered in the past and found herself looking down at the passing traffic, chilled and uncomforted.

How unfair to discover, after twelve years of dedication, that the shrines at which you'd worshipped housed empty gods. Only a fool, surely would have been deceived this long, for how else did you define a woman who deluded herself into believing she had found freedom only to discover, when the rose-tinted glasses came off, that she had nothing? What, in the end, did all her frantic acquisitions amount to—the business acclaim, the possessions, the all-important image?

What consolation was to be found in the remote and lifeless beauty of her fine antiques, now, when she finally acknowledged the extent of her loss? Why, in the

face of such consuming sorrow and regret, did the
glossy front she'd worn with such conviction crack
and drop away? What was it that was so damnably
precious that she'd weighed it up against Con and found
him somehow wanting?

Don't be so hard on yourself, her other half, the
fearful, selfish half, counselled. What is so strange
about the urge for self-preservation? Is it not, after all
the most basic instinct of humankind?

What is strange, the uncompromising voice of
conscience retorted, is that you should have become
such an abject coward, running blindly from all the
things that could have brought you happiness years
ago.

It wasn't my fault, she argued. My mother ... Con
... how was I to know?

What was it Con had said the last time she'd seen
him? 'It was your own fault ...' And it was, she saw
suddenly. Not just that she'd been penniless and ill, but
that she'd suffered at all. When was she going to take
charge of her own life and stop blaming other people
for her woes? Who was to blame but herself for the
mess she'd made with Con?

Willie had drawn her hair in two long veils around
her face, peering out at a world that threatened her with
its brave vitality. Liz had scorned such timidity. The
hair had gone—chop! The browns and khakis,
shapeless bags that defied her femininity, tossed out,
unfit, even, for the charity box on the supermarket
parking lot.

Liz, clever, sophisticated Liz, had no use for such
uninspired cowardice. She had taken glamour and
poise, dressed them in designer labels, doused them in
expensive French perfume, and teamed them with such
executive brilliance that she'd dazzled the whole world
and fooled them all—but especially herself—into
believing in what they saw. Why did it take Con's life
for her to see she'd merely exchanged one disguise for
another?

I am, she recognised dully, more impoverished now than I was then. I thought I had it all, but underneath, I am nothing; a mannequin masquerading as a woman; an illusion of female success who found out what womanliness was all about when it was too late.

Premonition encased her in such icy fear that even hunched under the quilt before the fire, she could not repress the shivers that rattled her frame. It was the cold of despair, for Con, she believed, would not be coming back.

Even Sam's determined optimism was beginning to pale. Ellen, though, had refused to dwell on such morbid suppositions and had refused to let Liz, either, which was why Liz had insisted her mother leave. Liz knew that, sooner or later, she'd have to face the knowledge that Con was . . . gone . . . lost . . .

Dead.

Drifting through to the hall, she looked in the mirror and said the word out loud to her reflection, heard the abbreviated finality of its sound, tried to absorb its meaning into her mind. And could not.

The only reality was the life that vibrated in Con. In his eyes, brilliantly blue, acutely observant, squinting against the sun, opaque with passion. In his body, lithe and energetic, superbly engineered, warm and vital. In his mind, alert, curious, leaping ahead, never idle, not even in sleep.

The laughter, the tenderness, even the anger, could not be gone. It was inconceivable. But death was a fact of life. It happened all the time. It was the only absolute.

She held her hands against her womb, protectively. Was this what immortality was all about? Continuity through new life? Had their own particular shining thread been severed?

The doorbell rang. Like a sleepwalker, she covered the distance to the door, and reached up heavy hands to pull it open. It was a monumental effort; she almost didn't bother, but at last it swung wide to reveal the visitor.

Con waited outside.

CHAPTER TWELVE

IN the slice of a second, he saw it all: the glazed misery in the eyes she raised to him, the blank, uncomprehending gaze indicative of the anguish that clamped her mind. Her pallor, alarming at first glance, intensified, washing the colour from her lips with frightening rapidity. Without a word, with scarcely time to release his pent-up breath, he crossed the threshold, kicking the door shut behind him, and reached out to absorb the deathly chill of despair that etched her features, pressing her to the warmth of him with fierce determination.

She was a rag doll in his arms, then strangely insubstantial, slipping like silent water through his fingers. Fearing she was about to faint, he sank with her to the floor, cushioning her against him until they rested together on the muted pastels of the Chinese rug in her entrance hall. Only then did he chance a second look at her, haunted by what he'd seen in her eyes a moment earlier.

But the pain was leaving, rained away by the glad tears that sprang from within where the hurt had been greatest.

'Oh, love, don't cry!' He bent over her and swept his lips over her eyelids, following the salty trails down her face, along her jaw. 'Don't . . .' he implored her, his voice thick with the alien congestion of his own emotion, '. . . please, don't let me make you cry again.'

He ran a gentle thumb over her chin and down her throat to the hollow at its base where a single tear had strayed and become trapped. And because they were so near and chilled, he stroked her collarbones too, and let his warm, dry palms slide beneath the loose velour robe she wore, to comfort the cool distress of her breasts and bring them surging back to life.

How frail she seemed, yet somehow ripe and luscious, too; half girl, half woman. 'I'm home,' he whispered against her mouth. 'It's all over; we're together again.'

But the words weren't enough. She was suspended in a net of fear, beyond his reach.

'Liz,' he begged, his hands pulling her urgently against him. She was there, with him, yet somehow absent, as if the spark that fired her vitality had been extinguished. 'Liz . . .' He pressed her to him, as if, by osmosis, he could inject her with the reality of him; flung one denim-clad leg over her hips and crushed her beneath its weight; buried his face in her hair, inhaling the fragrance of her with all the avid desperation of a man drawing his last breath.

Tugging at the robe, he sought to chafe life back into the body whose passivity terrified him. Where had his ardent, loving Liz gone? The buttons parted under his anxious ministrations, exposing the pale ivory of her limbs, the fine sweet curves of her that drove him to the brink of madness. How often, in the last three days, he'd sustained himself with the memory of her! To hold the reality now, in his arms, was a special sort of heaven.

He kissed her everywhere, hurried, scorching imprints that slid from the inner curve of her elbow to the sharp arc of her ribs, from the full undersides of her breasts to the soft swell of her belly, to merge at last in one all-encompassing embrace that brought a faint stirring of colour to her skin.

The need to feel her against his flesh, to banish with his warmth the lingering chill that tiptoed over her, took hold of him and would not be denied. And then, because he knew no other way to erase the source of her pain, he filled her with his slim, smooth strength and carried her away on the river of his love, rocking her, at last, in the liquid heat of exhausted passion.

'Oh, God!' He groaned, resting his forehead on one of the stylised pink roses that bordered the rug. 'Where's my mind at?' He lifted his head and gazed down at the bloom on her cheeks. 'Did I just do what I think I did? Am I a hopeless degenerate, or just your basic male animal?'

She reached up and smoothed back the hair that fell across his brow, then twined it through her fingers, marvelling at its—*his*—life. 'You're a hopeless, basic, degenerate male animal...' she whispered, trying desperately to match his wry humour, but it was too soon, and, to her shame, the easy tears swam in her eyes again. 'Why am I crying?' she quavered, then, at the remorse that sprang to his eyes, burst into fresh sobs. 'I'm so happy ... so grateful,' she wailed. All she wanted was to be able to extend her hand and be able to feel him close to her, to touch his dear face, to feel the vital warmth of him near her.

Cradling her in his arms, he carried her through to the living room and wrapped her in the quilt he found lying on the couch. 'I can be such an *ass*,' he murmured disgustedly. 'Such a total, complete ass. Why do you put up with me?'

'I love you.'

'Oh, my darling girl, I love you, too.' He squeezed his eyes shut in sudden agony. 'Please, *please*, let's be married. I know this isn't the right time, and I shouldn't press you; know there are things to tell you about the last few days, things we have to work out, but none of it matters except that I don't ever want to leave you again.'

The tears, the pain, and all the ragged fear evaporated. The weakness that had clung to her like an illness since she'd heard he was missing fell away and left her whole again. 'I'm so glad you asked,' she told him softly.

His eyes flew open, impossibly blue, haloed in those crazy lashes that always beguiled her so. 'Yes?'

'Oh, yes!'

She wanted to make him lunch, but he wouldn't let her. Instead, he rushed out and bought fresh chocolate croissants from the bakery down the block, and champagne from the liquor store nearby.

'Unconventional,' he admitted, setting everything before her on the coffee table where they'd once shared Chinese food, 'but definitely memorable, right?'

He poured two glasses of the wine and offered one to her. 'To our engagement,' he toasted. 'To ... what do they always say at weddings? ... a long and happy life.' He raised the glsss to his lips, then lowered it again, smiling at the radiance on her face. 'Oh Lord, I'm going to ravish you again! I can feel it coming on!'

'Before you do,' she said, placing her untouched glass on the table, 'there's something I have to say.' How pompous she sounded. She'd wanted to declare her pregnancy with flair, to present it to him like a gift, but all at once, she was tongue-tied, amazingly shy, unsure of the words to use.

'I'll respect you in the morning,' he promised, his wicked, endearing smile weaving unbreakable strings around her heart, and swept her dramatically to him, burrowing his lips into her neck. 'Tell me you'll be mine!' He was Dracula and Valentino rolled into one.

'I'm pregnant,' she announced baldly.

He recoiled from her, his arms falling away as though he'd gone to embrace a lover and found a boa constrictor instead. 'What?'

'Pregnant ...' she repeated uncertainly, trying to lever herself into a sitting position from where he'd dropped her back on the cushions. 'I'm going to have a baby, actually ...' Actually? a scornful inner voice enquired. Is there some other way to be pregnant the rest of the world hasn't heard about?

'... actually in about six months,' she amended nervously, and wondered if nurturing an unborn child depleted the intelligence of the mother. 'September ...'

'Honey, how can you be? You said before that you——'

'No. I thought I was sterile, but I was wrong, the doctors were wrong.'

'Are you sure? Have you seen another doctor?' He stopped, comprehension dawning. 'Doctor—of course!'

'Yes, but I didn't know for sure that day, Con,' she rushed to explain. 'He took tests and the results weren't ready till the next day, and by then you were up at the mill. I wasn't trying to keep it from you, honestly.'

'Oh, love, I know that.' He lifted her hands to his lips and kissed her fingers. 'And I'm so sorry for the things I said to you.'

'You had a right to be angry.'

'I had a right to be upset—for you, for both of us. I had no right to lash out at you. Liz, I spent the last three days going over what you told me, trying to put myself in your place. I feel ... humbled, I guess.'

'Never mind.' She laid her fingers across his lips. 'The point is, I can't drink the champagne, because I'm pregnant.'

He leaped to his feet with such vigour that a fearful agitation erupted among the contents of the table. The croissants trembled, and the champagne glasses teetered together, then rolled gracefully to the floor and emptied their expensive contents all over the ivory rug. 'Pregnant!' His exultation bounced off the walls, echoed, she was sure, throughout the building. 'Oh, my darling, clever, wonderful Liz!'

He swooped down again and made to gather her roughly into his arms, then stopped. 'Is it quite all right to ... touch you?' he asked anxiously, gazing at her in awe, and she laughed for the first time, it seemed, in weeks, a sound so filled with joy that he had to swallow the sudden lump that clogged his throat.

He made a fire and they spent the afternoon on the couch, talking about all the things that mattered, sweeping away all the cobwebs that lurked in the corners and cast shadows on their loving.

'We were never in any real danger,' he promised her, relating the events that led to his disappearance. 'We ran into foul weather and came down in one of the fjords, but the visibility was so bad, we hit something—a log or perhaps a rock—and damaged the pontoons on the plane. We just had time to get the life raft out and grab the emergency kit before she sank. We paddled ashore and waited out the storm, and at first light this morning, we were spotted by a Coastguard helicopter.'

'Why didn't Sam 'phone and let me know you'd been found?'

'He would have, love, but I was back in Vancouver in less than two hours and I wanted to come and show you I was okay, be here with you. Hell, telephones . . .' he kissed her, lingered over the sweet taste of her mouth, '. . . telephones,' he went on huskily, 'are for long-distance communiation.'

He had that look in his eye, and she felt her pulse leap in response.

'Are you glad about the baby?' he asked, much later. 'You sort of gave me the impression, at Whistler, that . . .'

'Oh Con, I feel like Elizabeth in the Bible. It's wonderful—a miracle. I can't wait to have him. I want at least two more.'

'Tell me everything the doctor said. Is he good? Can we trust him?'

'He's the best. Everything is fine and he's placing bets on delivering the baby on September the twentieth.'

'You know, don't you, that I want you for my wife whether you're pregnant or not? The marriage is strictly for us. We belong together.'

'That's what mother said. She was sure we'd work things out.'

'Ah, yes. The dragon lady. I'd like to wring her neck!' He scowled fiercely, drawing his brows together, then lifting them in disbelief. 'Don't tell me she's given her stamp of approval to our getting married?'

'In spades, darling.'

'The hell you say! What made her change her tune?'

'I guess she finally realised that what we shared was a lasting thing—not like her affair with my father.'

The hard line to Con's mouth gradually softened as she explained the circumstances surrounding her birth. 'Good God,' he muttered when she'd finished. 'The things we do sometimes to the people we claim to love! Did her father ever bother to check up on her, to make sure she was okay? Did he ever express an interest in his grandchild?'

'I didn't think so. He died a couple of years after I was born. I don't know what happened to the aunts.'

'Poor Ellen. This last week must have been pretty hard on her. Shall we call her up and tell her I'm going to make an honest woman out of you?'

'Could we go one better? Could we go over and tell her ourselves?'

'For you, my love,' he replied, drawing her to her feet and pulling her close, 'anything. But first . . .'

It was almost dark outside when Ellen opened her door to them. 'Oh!' She dabbed happily at her eyes and gave Con an awkward kiss. 'I'm very pleased for you both, and so happy you're safe, Con.'

'Thank you.' He hesitated fractionally. 'I'd like to marry your daughter, Mrs Newman.'

For a moment, Ellen's obsession with niceties surfaced. 'I should hope so—in her condition.'

'Mother!'

'Oh, I'm sorry, Willie. Con, forgive me, please.'

His smile, lethal with charm, dazzled her across the space separating them. 'No forgiveness required. We all make mistakes,' he assured her gallantly, and Liz watched, amused, as her mother succumbed without so much as a struggle.

'Why,' Ellen gasped, 'what a nice man you really are, after all.'

Con laughed, delighted.

'I was just trying to protect Willie, you know.'

He stretched his legs and eased himself to a more comfortable position in the spindly little chair to which he'd been assigned. 'Tell me something, Ellen.' He slanted laughing eyes at her where she presided over the tea tray. '*Where* did you find your daughter's names?'

'From my aunts. I thought, since they were such upright, strong-minded creatures, it might influence her moral character. Obviously, it didn't.' She dropped him a sly wink. 'Too much like her mother, I guess.'

Con choked quietly into his teacup.

Willie's wedding dress, Ellen observed approvingly, was beautifully *discreet*. The dropped waist quite disguised the decided thickening of her daughter's middle. Most suitable.

Her wedding outfit, Liz thought, as she gave herself a last inspection in the mirror, was an inspired confection. Blushing cream chiffon, falling in pleated layers from her hips to mid-calf, and topped by a cartwheel hat of the same colour. Violets, still damp with dew, nestled at the brim, matching those in the bouquet that Janice was holding out to her.

'Everyone is here,' she told Liz, giving her a hug that conveyed all her affection without disturbing a hair on either of their heads. 'Ready when you are.'

It was late April, and a lovely soft day. Con's

house—their home from now on, she reminded herself—was a dream. Old and gracious with leaded glass and fine wood panelling, it sat next to the ocean on beautifully landscaped grounds. The perfect setting, they'd decided, to celebrate their small, informal wedding. The rooms were full of flowers, the trees outside heavy with blossom.

'I brought rice to throw,' Janice confided, then shot Liz a dark glare. 'Cooked rice! I'll never forgive you for snagging old Bedroom Eyes from under my nose.' She swept ahead of Liz, out to where the guests were assembled, nodding sunnily, and blithely unconcerned with the bride's sudden attack of choking mirth.

Scanning the length of the room, her gaze fell on where the tall, darkly handsome groom waited in sober black—sober, that was, until she flicked a glance at his face. Oh, those eyes! Devouring Liz, undressing her in unashamed hunger as she made her slow way towards him!

Preceding Liz, Janice reached the place where Con waited, then turned to watch the bride take the final steps that brought her to her groom. *This* was a marriage made in heaven. She blinked, furious at the prick of tears that threatened her carefully applied mascara, and turned away. It seemed an indecent intrusion to observe the look he bestowed on his bride.

Turning to face her as he began the vows that would unite them before the whole world, Con paused a moment, arrested by the beauty and serenity of her. It was more than just the radiant face of a bride. She was like something out of one of the museums of Europe: Madonna With Violets, he thought fancifully. And that dress! Another creation calculated to make a man crazy with wanting what it so slyly concealed!

Reaching out to take her hand in his sure, firm grasp, he let his gaze linger briefly on her body, the lowered sweep of his lashes hiding the surge of love and passion that inflamed his eyes, deepening them to pure, rich cobalt.

'I, Conroy, take you, Elizabeth . . .'

Harlequin Presents

Coming Next Month

911 TO FILL A SILENCE Jayne Bauling
Bustling Taipei sets the scene for a reunion between a free-lance radio reporter and her celebrated ex-husband. He's still as charming and impulsive as ever—the sort of man who'd marry on a whim.

912 TITAN'S WOMAN Ann Charlton
When a powerful Australian developer gives in to a woman's concern for the environment, the newspapers dub them "TITAN and the Amazon." Then he, an experienced infighter, goes straight for the heart!

913 HUNTER'S PREY Jasmine Cresswell
For two years a runaway wife has fled from city to city, state to state, to hide herself and her child from the only man she's ever loved. And now he's found her....

914 WHAT'S RIGHT Melinda Cross
A powerful force draws an interior designer to a wealthy American businessman, though a tragic sense of loyalty binds him to another. But his determination to do what's right only makes her love him more.

915 CHANCE MEETINGS Vanessa James
A man—a rich man—is needed to save her family's Cornish estate. And just like that, two marriageable men happen along—one for Caro and one for her cousin. But nothing's so easy....

916 FIRE WITH FIRE Penny Jordan
When a London newscaster sacrifices everything but her ethics to repay a wily entrepreneur for her sister's recklessness, it occurs to him that he could use a woman like her in his life.

917 A RISKY BUSINESS Sandra K. Rhoades
Risks come with the territory for an Alberta oil scout. But she doesn't plan to risk her heart—not until she's caught snooping around a self-made millionaire's oilfields.

918 LIKE ENEMIES Sophie Weston
With ten-year-old headlines of the family scandal still etched in her mind, a London designer is frightened and confused by her feelings for an alluring international businessman.

Available in September wherever paperback books are sold, or through Harlequin Reader Service:

In the U.S.
P.O. Box 1397
Buffalo, N.Y.
14240-1397

In Canada
P.O. Box 2800, Postal Station A
5170 Yonge Street
Willowdale, Ontario M2N 6J3

Could she find love as a mail-order bride?

MARIANNE WILLMAN

PIECES OF SKY

In the Arizona of 1873, Nora O'Shea is caught between life with a contemptuous, arrogant husband and her desperate love for Roger LeBeau, half-breed Comanche Indian scout and secret freedom fighter.

═══ OFFICIAL RULES ═══

Harlequin "Super Celebration" SWEEPSTAKES

NEW PRIZES—NEW PRIZE FEATURES & CHOICES—MONTHLY

1. To enter the sweepstakes, follow the instructions outlined on the Center Insert Card. Alternate means of entry, NO PURCHASE NECESSARY, you may also enter by mailing your name, address and birthday on a plain 3″ x 5″ piece of paper to: In U.S.A.: Harlequin "Super Celebration" Sweepstakes, P.O. Box 1867, Buffalo, N.Y. 14240-1867. In Canada: Harlequin "Super Celebration" Sweepstakes, P.O. Box 2800, 5170 Yonge Street, Postal Station A, Willowdale, Ontario M2N 6J3.

2. Winners will be selected in random drawings from all entries received. All prizes will be awarded. These prizes are in addition to any free gifts which might be offered. Versions of this sweepstakes with different prizes may appear in other presentations by TorStar and their affiliates. The maximum value of the prizes offered is $8,000.00. Winners selected will receive the prize offered from their prize package.

3. The selection of winners will be conducted under the supervision of Marden-Kane, an independent judging organization. By entering the sweepstakes, each entrant accepts and agrees to be bound by these rules and the decision of the judges which shall be final and binding. Odds of winning are dependent upon the total number of entries received. Taxes, if any, are the sole responsibility of the winners. Prizes are not transferable. This sweepstakes is scheduled to appear in Retail Outlets of Harlequin Books during the period of June 1986 to December 1986. All entries must be received by January 31st, 1987. The drawing will take place on or about March 1st, 1987 at the offices of Marden-Kane, Lake Success, New York. For Quebec (Canada) residents, any litigation regarding the running of this sweepstakes and the awarding of prizes must be submitted to La Regie de Lotteries et Course du Quebec.

4. This presentation offers the prizes as illustrated on the Center Insert Card.

5. This offer is open to residents of the U.S., and Canada, 18 years or older, except employees of TorStar, its affiliates, subsidiaries, Marden-Kane and all other agencies and persons connected with conducting this sweepstakes. All Federal, State and local laws apply. Void where prohibited or restricted by law. Winners will be notified by mail and may be required to execute an affidavit of eligibility and release which must be returned within 14 days after notification. Winners consent to the use of their name, photograph and/or likeness for advertising and publicity in conjunction with this and similar promotions without additional compensation. One prize per family or household. Canadian winners will be required to answer a skill testing question.

6. For a list of our most recent prize winners, send a stamped, self-addressed envelope to: WINNERS LIST, c/o Marden-Kane, P.O. Box 525, Sayreville, NJ 08872.

No Lucky Number needed to win!

HARLEQUIN HISTORICAL

Explore love with Harlequin in the Middle
Ages, the Renaissance, in the Regency, the
Victorian and other eras.

Relive within these books the endless ages of
romance, set against authentic historical
backgrounds. Two new historical love stories
published each month.